The Undaunted Bride

Miranda Cameron

A SIGNET BOOK

NEW AMERICAN LIBRARY

NAL BOOKS ARE AVAILABLE AT QUANTITY DISCOUNTS WHEN USED TO
PROMOTE PRODUCTS OR SERVICES. FOR INFORMATION PLEASE WRITE
TO PREMIUM MARKETING DIVISION, NEW AMERICAN LIBRARY,
1633 BROADWAY, NEW YORK, NEW YORK 10019.

SIGNET TRADEMARK REG. U.S. PAT. OFF. AND FOREIGN COUNTRIES
REGISTERED TRADEMARK—MARCA REGISTRADA.
HECHO EN CHICAGO, U.S.A.

SIGNET, SIGNET CLASSIC, MENTOR, ONYX, MERIDIAN and
NAL BOOKS are published by New American Library,
1633 Broadway, New York, New York 10019

First Printing, March, 1987

PRINTED IN THE UNITED STATES OF AMERICA

One

The curricle rattled along the winding Devon country road at breakneck speed. Beatrice, holding on to her blue hat lest it be blown away by the cold wind of the moors, glanced uneasily at the stern, swarthy profile of her husband.

"There is no need to drive with such haste," she remonstrated with him. "We might overturn."

In answer Lord Brook cracked his whip and the curricle jolted on even faster. "The sooner you become accustomed to my ways, the better," he said through his teeth.

Beatrice pushed away a stray curl of her glossy black hair with an irritated gesture. "I shan't become accustomed to folly, nor do I wish to," she snapped, her deep blue eyes clouding with anger. "*You* may be considered a great whip, but *I* have no fancy to land in the ditch with a broken head."

The baron cast her a cold look of dislike. "You can be sure that I don't wish to end up with a broken head either," he retorted. "I don't know what is worse, a lachrymose timid schoolgirl who hardly opens her mouth" (an obvious allusion to her friend Evelyn), "or a headstrong pert female who opens hers much too often. Females," he added bitterly, "are all dreadful creatures." His thin mouth snapped shut to a grim line, and his brooding black eyes burned with suppressed hatred.

Beatrice's smooth white brow furrowed in puzzlement. "It is a pity then that you were obliged to tie yourself to one of them," she retorted, realizing with a sudden start that she knew very little about her husband. Their glittering London wedding had only made him cross. If it had been up to him, they would have been married in a little church on the moor. Now, five days into their marriage, he was still out of temper.

He should complain, thought Beatrice with a wry twist to her mouth. What about her own plans and dreams? Her heart contracted at the memory of her heartache and loss. But she had resigned herself to her fate and was determined to make the best of it. She had not expected it to be *that* difficult. Nor had she expected her husband to leave his house immediately after they had arrived there.

She was beginning now to comprehend Evelyn's feelings. Evelyn, whose papa was Lord Brook's good friend, disliked Lord Brook. And disliked Dartmoor even more, wondering that the baron should choose to live in such a wild and desolate place.

Wild it certainly was, Beatrice conceded, scanning the rolling heather-covered hills topped with gigantic gray stones in weird shapes. The landscape was more desolate to the west. To the east, the lush valley of a river divided the heather-covered slopes.

But signs of new growth enlivened even the desolate landscape. Patches of emerald green and the yellow blooms of gorse bushes were a welcome sight. As were the bluebells and other spring flowers by the road, some scenting with their fragrance the bracing air of the moor. Moor ponies and sheep grazed here and there, and some birds flew occasionally overhead.

Beatrice wished Lord Brook would let *her* drive, but she knew it would be useless to ask him. He had not responded to her last comment; his dark brooding eyes were fixed on the road.

She glanced again at his grim countenance, at the thick straight brows, the deep lines running from the corners of his nose to his mouth, the cleft chin. Gareth Christopher Risborough, Lord Brook, was not considered a handsome man, but Beatrice thought his face revealed manliness and strength. And no one could find fault with his figure. He was a tall, broad-shouldered man of six-and-thirty, lean and hard-muscled, and impeccably attired as a gentleman of fashion, though not a dandy.

Now a stylish beaver hat covered his short raven hair, his cravat was stiffly starched and intricately tied, and his many-caped buff driving coat offered much better protection against the wind than her light blue velvet pelisse.

She heaved an inward sigh. If only his disposition were a trifle different, she thought. What was he thinking now? she mused, watching the taut line of his mouth.

It was as well she could not read his thoughts, for not all of them were flattering to her. Perhaps he should instead have chosen the watering pot, Evelyn, the baron was reflecting.

But a lifetime spent in the company of a hysterical female was not to be contemplated. He had enough of that from his sister, Albinia, forever moaning and having palpitations or vapors. Also, Evelyn was only nineteen, while Beatrice was twenty-six, therefore preferable in his eyes. It was only at the wedding reception that he had discovered Beatrice possessed a temper and a strong will.

She had seemed a diamond of the first water, too. A delightful face and figure. Elegant dress and carriage, and strikingly beautiful deep blue eyes. But in them and in the cut of her chin he could read determination.

Determination, bah! Stubbornness. That's what it was. He had no wish to take her with him, but she had insisted on coming along.

As his anger welled up anew, his attention wandered, and the horses took the turn in the road a trifle too fast. Beatrice gave a slight cry as the curricle careened and almost, it seemed to her, overturned. "My lord, pray take care," she cried. "Pray drive more slowly."

His lips twisted in a cynical curl. "You wished to come with me, ma'am," he countered in a biting voice. "You have only yourself to blame if the ride is not to your liking."

The man was mad, thought Beatrice, releasing her breath, thankful that the curricle was still in an upright position. Setting out from Brook Manor, he had driven fast enough to cause his old groom to admonish him, but *that* had been a sedate pace compared with his present speed. Yet she fancied a few times a spasm of pain had crossed his features. She wished she dared to question him about it, though the explanation seemed obvious. Being such a reckless driver, he must have taken at least one tumble or maybe more, which had caused him some lasting injury. Folly, utter folly, she thought with contempt. At least Edgar, his nephew, appeared to be of a different cut.

Edgar, concerned and worried, deplored his uncle's reckless driving, but could not persuade him to reason, and only received cutting remarks for his pains.

Her heart warmed at the thought of this handsome light-haired man, only a few years younger than her husband. *He* had treated Beatrice with only friendliness and respect.

Another bend in the road was not far off, but Lord Brook obviously had no intention of slackening his pace. Reckless driving, it seemed, was his way of venting his spleen. Beatrice was debating with herself whether it would be of any use to remonstrate with him again, when suddenly and quite unexpectedly the mist rolled in over the moors.

It was most singular and eerie. One moment, it seemed, the view was clear on both sides of the road, and the next, all was shrouded in a heavy fog. And it wasn't even evening.

Beatrice shivered, because the dampness made the cold wind feel worse, and drew her pelisse more closely around her. Certainly *now* he must slacken the pace.

She should have known better. "My lord, surely you cannot continue in this fashion in the mist," she protested.

"I know the road well," he answered curtly, without turning his head.

Of all the mutton-headed men, he was the worst. Beatrice found it hard to keep a civil tongue in her head. "You are the most obstinate, stubborn, opinionated man of my acquaintance, and it would serve you right if we overturned," she cried. "Except I have no wish to suffer a fall."

He ignored this remark, but that he did not appreciate it was shown by the twitching of a muscle at his jaw and by his tightly pressed lips.

The thick fog swirled about them, creeping closer. The turn of the road, very near, was hardly visible. And he will drive on at this pace, Beatrice thought in despair.

Abruptly and without warning, but a short distance away from them and from the turn, an animal shape emerged out of the mist in the middle of the narrow road.

"Take care," Beatrice screamed. "A sheep on the road."

But Lord Brook was already attempting to check the grays' gallop. Exercising great skill, he contrived to slow their pace, yet was unable to bring the curricle to a standstill.

To Beatrice, her heart in her mouth, hanging on to

the seat of the curricle for dear life, everything seemed to happen all at once. The horses shied, reared up and snorted, doing their best to overturn the vehicle. Incredibly, Lord Brook swung to one side, driving past the animal with a hairbreadth to spare, but the wheels struck a stone by the road. The curricle sustained a severe jolt. And Lord Brook, with a sharp cry, was thrown out of the carriage.

Two

Beatrice watched in horror as her husband toppled over into the mist. But even as her mind was registering this shocking act, her body acted instantaneously. She grabbed at the reins, and utilizing all her strength and skill, managed to bring the vehicle to a standstill.

Jumping nimbly from the carriage, she ran to the horses' heads to calm them; then, hoping they would not bolt, she rushed back to Lord Brook's inanimate body on the road.

By the time she dropped to her knees beside him, he was stirring and opening his eyes. His beaver hat had fallen off, and blood matted his hair and his brow, but the wound was not bleeding much. There might, however, be a concussion.

"My lord, are you badly hurt?" she cried. "Is anything broken?"

He shook his head, wincing, and tried to sit up. "So much for my reputation as an excellent whip," he said, his lips curling in self-derision. "Falling off the seat like the veriest Johnny Raw."

Beatrice, supporting his shoulders, cautioned, "Perhaps you ought to remain prone until we make sure that nothing is broken."

"Nothing is broken," he muttered weakly but irritably. "The grays," he abruptly recollected.

"They have sustained no harm," Beatrice reassured him.

His brow furrowed. "As I recall, I didn't—"

"I contrived to stop them."

He looked up with dawning respect. "I make you my compliments." He frowned again. "I could have controlled them. This wouldn't have happened if—" He bit his lip and tried to push himself up, only to cry out suddenly, clutch at his right arm, and fall back deathly pale.

Beads of perspiration bathed his brow. His teeth clamped on his lower lip and his dark eyes clouded with pain.

Beatrice lowered him gently to the ground. "It *is* broken," she said.

"It is not," he muttered. "It just . . . hurts."

"But . . ." She shook her head. The voluminous folds of his driving coat made an examination of his hurts exceedingly difficult. She cradled his head in her lap, and pulling out her smelling salts from the reticule attached at her waist, uncorked the bottle and waved it under his nose.

He coughed. "Take it away, I haven't swooned. Damnation." He stirred and bit his lip.

"Pray, do not move. Let me bandage your head," said Beatrice.

Using her handkerchief for a pad and his cravat to tie it with, she fashioned a bandage. "It needs to be washed and properly tended to," she said worriedly.

He had shut his eyes as she performed her ministrations, and remained thus motionless with lips tightly pressed for a while after she had finished. Then his eyes blinked open. He took a deep breath and cautiously tried to move his legs and arms.

The left leg appeared to give him some trouble, but it wasn't broken. *That* Beatrice could ascertain. No swelling, and it looked normal. He could move his left arm without too much trouble. Only the right arm was hurting him a great deal, for each time he moved it, he bit on his lip and lost color. But he reassured Beatrice that it wasn't broken.

"This arm gives me trouble now and then. And falling off the curricle wasn't likely to improve its condition," he explained, to her relief.

He glanced at the ever-thickening mist that now obscured everything a yard away from them. "I must see to the grays," he muttered. "Damnation, I shouldn't have dismissed Hickley, my groom. But I was tired of his nagging. He knew me when I was a boy, and thinks he can take liberties."

"No need to fret. Even if they bolt, Hickley shall find them for you. What worries me is that another vehicle might come along, and in this fog the driver might not see us."

The baron, agreeing with her, gritted his teeth and sat up, then, reluctantly accepting her help, staggered to his feet. His face was pale and drawn.

Beatrice thought the sooner his hurts could be attended to, the better; but she realized it would require both her and Hickley's efforts to assist him into the carriage. Hickley was following them on horseback and should catch up with them presently. Meanwhile she would help her husband off the road and see to the curricle and horses.

With her aid the baron stumbled to the side of the road. Beatrice, finding a handy boulder, was helping him to sit down, when he put up his hand. "Listen, I hear hoofbeats."

Beatrice pricked up her ears. Muffled by the fog, the sound of horses' hooves could indeed be heard, and soon the shape of a rider loomed out of the mist.

"Hickley." Lord Brook sighed with relief.

The next moment the squat groom swung himself from his horse and ran up to them. "Milord, are you hurt?" he cried.

"Nothing to signify," said his master irritably. "See to the horses."

The groom shook his grizzly head. "I suspicioned something like that would happen. So I took it upon myself to hasten after your lordship with all speed."

"Indeed I am very grateful you did, Hickley," said Beatrice. "I do think his lordship did not sustain a lasting injury, but he must be helped into the carriage."

The groom shook his head. "The curricle won't do his lordship no good. He needs a chaise. A posting inn is but a short ride away. Be pleased to wait with his lordship, milady. I'll fetch a chaise."

"The grays," said the baron faintly, but with annoyance.

"Don't you fret, your lordship, I'll see to them," said the groom. He touched his cap. "I shall be back in a trice." And he jumped on his horse and disappeared into the mist.

Beatrice perched on the boulder beside Lord Brook.

"Pray shut your eyes, my lord, and rest. You shall be more comfortable that way."

He did not respond, and at first sat stiffly erect, but presently his body sagged and he relaxed against her shoulder. Beatrice felt his full weight, but was glad to be of help. She wished she had some water to bathe his brow. There must be water aplenty here. The ground smelled of wetness, and even here by the side of the road her feet sank deep into the soggy soil. But she dared not look for clear water in this mist.

She gave an inward sigh. This indeed was not a very propitious beginning to her marriage, she thought wryly. Still, none of this should matter to her. After all, their marriage was just one of convenience, and he was her husband in name only. And however crotchety and disagreeable he could be, he was only six-and-thirty and infinitely preferable as a husband to a fat, gouty squire of fifty-six. Which was the alternate choice her family had given her.

If only she had not been obliged to marry. For a long time she had resisted her parents' attempts to arrange an advantageous marriage for her, but now the situation had come to *point non plus* and debtors' prison stared them all in the face. And Beatrice with disgust and reluctance had agreed to marry a man of means. She, who had vowed to marry only for love. Though she had had many suitors at her come-out, none had caught her fancy. And the man she was in love with, she was not allowed to marry.

Roderick was a baronet's second son, with no fortune or expectations, so was not considered by her parents and brother a suitable *parti* for Beatrice. Her lips twisted at the painful recollection. So poor Roderick had enlisted, gone to fight against Napoleon, and was killed. Beatrice told herself she had gotten over the loss and the hurt but did not think it very likely she would ever fall in love again. And was determined to remain a spinster. Until now.

Her husband, of course, had no need to make an advantageous alliance. He was a man of considerable fortune. All the more surprising, then, that it was so important to him to inherit his maternal grandfather's estate. It was to fullfill the conditions of the will, in order to inherit Tavis Hall, that he had been obliged to marry, and to marry yet this spring.

Sir Guy's estate was so important to him that hardly had they arrived at Brook Manor from London than he set out for Tavis Hall to claim it. They were returning now to the manor after inspecting the estate.

Beatrice thought back to her wedding. Not many of her husband's friends attended it. And those who did, behaved in a strangely cold way. Perfectly polite, but distant. Only one or two seemed to be genuinely fond of him and had greeted him warmly. And the rest of the *ton* seemed to be, yes, hostile to him, if not cutting him outright.

Perhaps his morose disposition was to blame for this, she reasoned. Perhaps he did not even bother to invite all his friends, since obviously this marriage was distasteful to him. If she had known . . . She shrugged. No use thinking of that.

As if divining her thoughts, the baron suddenly spoke up stiffly without opening his eyes. "I must beg your pardon for this fiasco. To be sure, you had insisted on coming with me, but you certainly did not bargain on *this*. Normally it would not have occurred. I wouldn't have . . . I should . . . I . . ."

Beatrice was agreeably surprised. From Evelyn's talk and from her own brief experience she had concluded that he never regarded the sensibilities of others.

She suppressed her urge to say: I told you this would happen. "Don't fret," she said instead in a calm voice. "It can happen to anybody, even to the best of whips."

His eyes flew open. "I . . . I am quite conscious of your taking the whole incident in such good spirit," he said as if forcing the words out. "I . . . Oh, damnation." His eyes flashed with annoyance and anger. "We both made a bargain—at least your father made one for you. There is no need to make the situation worse for ourselves."

"None whatsoever," Beatrice agreed cordially, her countenance expressing her surprise and approbation. Amazing, he had said more in this short space of time than in all of their brief acquaintance.

"Where is that damned chaise?" He fretted, moved and winced, but waved away her concerned exclamation.

"Beatrice, I . . ." His mouth tightened. He swallowed, then took a deep breath. "I am not an easy man to live with, but I shan't restrict your life. Within reason, you may do as you please. But do recall that Devon, and especially Dartmoor, isn't London. What might be condoned there would be frowned upon here, and what is frowned upon even by the *ton* is considered a deadly crime here. And don't I know it. So take care. For myself, I ask only one thing." He paused. "Fidelity."

Beatrice had listened to him with growing appreciation, but at this last word she bristled. "I beg your pardon. Surely you cannot imply that I can be capable of . . . of . . ." Words failed her.

He said irritably, the muscle at his jaw working, "I cannot know what you are capable of. Females can be capable of anything. For all I know, and for all your being headstrong and outspoken, you might be incapable of baseness and deceit. I don't know. I am willing to give you the benefit of the doubt. I do know that whereas Evelyn would never do anything improper because of her timidity and inculcated sense of values, I can wager that you could do anything you set your mind to. Whether you *would* is another matter. And recall, your papa is not my good friend, merely an acquaintance. I don't know your family well at all."

"Then why have you chosen me over Evelyn?" asked Beatrice, nettled. Her lips curved in a half-amused, half-cynical smile, recalling how her papa and Evelyn's father had vied with each other to bring his lordship up to scratch.

"I have an aversion to vapors," Lord Brook said shortly. "And . . . and . . ." He paused, then said, his face and voice expressionless, "I was struck by your beauty, grace, and address. A man could do worse than choosing you."

"I thank you for the compliment," Beatrice said, not knowing whether to be angry or gratified.

"One more thing . . ." He broke off and frowned.

He could not speak of it to her now. Perhaps when they were better acquainted. They had separate bed-chambers, of course, and it was understood that he would not force himself upon her. But what if the child should die before him, and Edgar then stepped into his shoes after his death? Unthinkable.

He should have considered that possibility before. Though there was no reason to suppose the child would die. It was healthy enough, and he would ensure the little boy and his mother the best of care and protection. He pushed the vexing thoughts aside and tried to relax, but time dragged on for him exceedingly slowly.

The muffled sound of hoofbeats and the rattle of wheels heralded an approaching carriage. "The chaise, at last." The baron sighed with relief.

And indeed it was the chaise.

A few moments later, amid the worried cluckings of his groom, the baron was assisted into the chaise, and they continued their journey. They would halt at the nearest posting inn, to have Lord Brook's wound attended to, before proceeding to Brook Manor.

Beatrice, cold and tired, ensuring only that her husband was made as comfortable as he could be, shut her eyes and let weariness of body and mind overcome her. She hoped her husband had not hurt himself too much, and she hoped the atmosphere at the manor would be more congenial than on her first arrival.

Perhaps, somewhat apprehensive and suffering from the strain of the wedding and the journey from London, she had fancied everything worse than it was. After all, Beatrice could get along with most people, and she was not about to put herself forward or usurp Lord Brook's sister's place. And if he made no demands on her, perhaps she would find life at Brook Manor unobjectionable.

So she reasoned. But events proved otherwise.

Three

Sometime later, the baron, restored to strength in a posting inn, his head wound washed and covered with sticking plaster, was being helped into the carriage once more. He was minus his greatcoat, but his dove-gray pantaloons and bottle-green coat were cleaned off, as were Beatrice's blue sprigged-muslin gown and her pelisse.

The fog had lifted as they resumed their journey to Brook Manor, and the view on both sides of the road was quite clear.

But the scenery this time seemed to Beatrice bleak and severe. The narrow road twisted between what now looked to her like vast stretches of boulder-strewn barren wasteland. Perhaps this impression was caused by the creeping shadows which made everything look gray and lifeless. Only some bracken and gorse bushes here and there were discernible, and the last rays of the setting sun silhouetted the huge outcroppings of granite, the weird-shaped gray stones, called tors. They seemed to her now like evil sentinels guarding their severe domain from too-bold trespassers. She shivered as the cold wind of the moor, which had picked up, penetrated her velvet pelisse to her thin muslin gown.

She shook her head impatiently. What was the matter with her? She was entering into Evelyn's sentiments about the moor. Something she never thought she would do. Her nerves must still be overset from the accident with the curricle and her talk with Lord Brook. Still, the scenery on this stretch of the moor was more wild and desolate. They passed several circles of stones along the way—the remnants of abodes of prehistoric men, people who roamed and lived on this moor thousands of years ago. Even then they preferred this brooding, forbidding, and sinister place for their habitation, as did the ancestors of Lord Brook.

As they continued their journey, Beatrice kept glancing at her husband from time to time. He seemed to have dozed off. Only the occasional twitch of the muscle at his jaw, the tightening of his lips, showed that he was not asleep. Was he in pain? She hesitated to ask him, to disturb his rest.

The road went up and up, until it topped a rise, and the vast panorama of the desolate heather-covered rolling slopes was spread before her. And the sun had set just then. The shadows on the ground deepened.

The moor road made yet another turn, then joined a side road which would bring them to Brook Manor. A steep descent along this road led toward the clump of trees against which was silhouetted the great stone house enclosed by a garden and a stone wall.

The mansion, its windows ablaze with light, was quite discernible from the road and the moor. Lord Brook's ancestor who had built this abode loved the moor so much that he wished to have an unobstructed view of it. Hence the park and the woods were at the back of the house. Only a garden, with just a few trees, fronted the house, and the low stone wall was interrupted in front by a free-standing gatehouse with twin towers, capped by strange cupolas, called ogees.

Brook Manor was a sprawling edifice, built around a courtyard, the central structure in the Tudor style, with many high chimneys, steep rooftops, and gables, and mullioned windows. Beatrice now understood that the lights streaming through all the windows were not for their benefit, but were due to Edgar's fear of the dark. Like Lord Byron, Edgar slept with a lighted taper in his room, and could not bear to walk about dark corridors and chambers. Lord Brook, to Beatrice's indignation, had only contempt for Edgar's fear. As if the poor man could help it. But Lord Brook, apparently possessing a fearless nature, was intolerant of the fears of others.

The chaise rolled down the steep incline toward the manor.

Beatrice glanced uneasily at her husband. He had straightened up and was staring at the edifice with what Beatrice fancied in the dim light was a cynical curl of his lip. "Edgar is still in residence," he said with contempt. "I was hoping he would absent himself again."

A sharp comment rose to Beatrice's lips, but she bit it back. What would be the purpose? Lord Brook obviously disliked his nephew excessively, and no amount of talk on her part would make him change his mind.

The post chaise, followed by the curricle, passed through the gates into the wide lane with lawns on both sides, and rolled along the carriage sweep to the front porch—a tall structure supported by columns. From inside it, through the front doors, a stream of light cut through the shadows. And as the post chaise halted, a footman ran up to open the door and let down the steps. Beatrice, glancing anxiously at her husband, hesitated.

"Pray alight," he cried irritably.

The footman helped Beatrice to descend, then helped her husband.

Lord Brook offered Beatrice his arm. But he seemed not quite steady on his feet, and it was Beatrice who supported him into the house. It was not something he accepted with pleasure, but evidently he preferred her supporting arm to that of the footman, whose help he declined.

His doctor should be sent for, thought Beatrice, but kept her own counsel for the moment.

As before, on their entering the musty great hall with its paintings, ancient weapons, and stags' heads on the walls, Beatrice found it brightly lit. The many candles in wall sconces and the chandelier dispelled the gloom of the dark oak paneling and of the soot-darkened large beams of the ceiling.

Pedmore, the stately gray-haired butler, was coming toward them across the black-and-white-checkered stone floor. For an instant his impassive countenance betrayed concern on seeing the baron holding on to Beatrice's arm. The concern quickly vanished, to be replaced by a wooden, expressionless mask.

"It is good to see you back, my lord, my lady." He bowed. And no doubt he wished to add, "in one piece."

The rustle of Mrs. Teswick's stiff black dress heralded her approach even before Beatrice caught sight of her. The housekeeper was a tall, gray-haired woman of indeterminate age and rigid straight carriage. While Pedmore and the footman bustled about them, Mrs. Teswick sent a sharp, hostile glance at Beatrice out of cold gray eyes.

"Shall Dr. Maynard be fetched?" she asked in a toneless voice, consulting the watch she had pinned to her ample bosom. "I fancy I know where he can be reached."

"Pray do so," and "No," said Beatrice and Lord Brook almost at the same time, the baron releasing his hold on Beatrice.

"But, my lord, your wound must be properly looked after," protested Beatrice.

He glared at her and would have spoken up, when Edgar Lindfield rushed forward from a door at the back of the hall, his trim figure elegant in primrose pantaloons and olive-green coat. The welcoming smile froze on his countenance as he beheld the sticking plaster.

"Oh, uncle," he cried with concern and reproach, "you must have driven or ridden in that neck-or-nothing fashion again. You know you can no longer indulge in such pastimes. I had hoped you could persuade him to be more careful," he said to Beatrice.

The baron's lips pressed into a grim, forbidding line. The muscle at his jaw twitched, and his dark eyes flashed with anger. "Disappointed again, Edgar?" he said through shut teeth, while Edgar spread his hands in a helpless gesture.

"Oh, pray don't, my lord," cried Beatrice, distressed. "He has your welfare at heart."

"You really think so?" said Lord Brook with a curling lip. "But then, females are always deceived by a handsome countenance and polished address."

"Must every person who is handsome, friendly, and polite be a deceiver?" Beatrice cried hotly.

Abruptly the baron swayed on his feet. Both Edgar and Beatrice rushed to support him. He evaded Edgar's grasp, clutching instead at Beatrice.

"The drawing room," said Edgar. "He should sit down."

Relieved of her pelisse, Beatrice felt suddenly cold. She shivered.

With a surprising show of strength, the baron straightened, took her arm, and treading with slow but firm steps, led her past one branch of the double carved oak staircase to the drawing room on the right. "Have a fire lit in the hall, Pedmore," he threw over his shoulder to the butler.

Beatrice could only admire his iron will, which commanded his hurt body to obey him. And she appreciated his instant concern about her comfort. If only he could rid himself of his strange prejudice against his nephew, she thought.

The drawing room, lit by the large chandelier, presented a friendly appearance, the red Axminster carpet and the crimson damask upholstery adding to the feeling of cheeriness. Only the tall, willowy, middle-aged woman in a mauve silk gown, swathed in a multitude of mauve and silver shawls, and enveloped in a cloud of lavender, did not fit into that cheerful picture. Though her blond hair, rather like Edgar's, was covered with a pretty cap of mauve lace tied with satin ribbons, and her comely pale countenance was still youthful-looking, the small mouth wore a petulant downward droop and the pale blue eyes expressed discontent and boredom.

This was Albinia Risborough, the baron's spinster sister and his only other living relation.

"At last," she exclaimed. "I had almost given you up, Brook. You said you were re—" Albinia's jaw dropped and she smote her slim hands together. "The sticking plaster! You fell again, riding or driving. Oh," she suddenly moaned, clutching at her bosom. "How can you be so inconsiderate? If you don't care about yourself, pray care about *my* delicate constitution. You know how even the slightest provocation is injurious to my health. As if your marrying Beatrice instead of Evelyn was not enough to overset my nerves. Must you add to my misery by agitating me with your heedless carelessness? Oh, I shall have a spasm."

Anger and hurt welled up in Beatrice at Albinia's words. She certainly did not pretend she welcomed Beatrice into the family, but from their brief acquaintance Beatrice realized also that consideration of others was not one of Albinia's strong features.

The baron glared at his sister with irritation and disgust. At the same time, he again swayed slightly.

"Pray, uncle, you are not well. Pray take a seat." Edgar grabbed Lord Brook's arm, but Lord Brook snatched it away.

"Don't touch me. I don't need your solicitude," he

said harshly, a sneer twisting his thin lips. Beneath his dark complexion he lost color.

Beatrice glanced anxiously at her husband. "Do sit down and rest, my lord," she said with concern. "And pray allow me to explain to your sister while you rest." But he didn't have to snap Edgar's nose off, she thought.

The baron stumbled to a red velvet armchair by the fireplace and collapsed into it, the pallor on his countenance increasing.

Edgar pulled imperiously on the bell rope. Pedmore himself appeared at once, as if waiting behind the door (listening at the keyhole, if that had not been beneath his dignity).

"Fetch some restorative at once, Pedmore," Edgar said. "And send someone to fetch Dr. Maynard, if Mrs. Teswick has not done so already."

"Damn you, Edgar. Stop fussing," cried Lord Brook, but a spasm of pain crossed his features. "I don't need the doctor."

"I beg to differ, uncle. I do think Dr. Maynard must be sent for." He shook his head sadly. "One of these days you shall have a tumble from which you shan't recover."

"*He* shan't recover? *I* shan't recover," moaned Albinia, sinking back against the cushions and groping for her vinaigrette. "Oh, doesn't anybody around here consider *my* feelings, *my* sensibilities? Oh, how inconsiderate of you, Brook, inconveniencing us all with your folly."

If she had not been worried about her husband, Beatrice would have been diverted by his sister's "injured sensibilities."

"Pray lean back and shut your eyes, my lord," she said, disregarding Albinia's lamentations. "You shall be better directly." She deftly picked up the vinaigrette from the sofa before Albinia's fingers could touch it, and crossing over to her husband, waved it under his nose.

He had leaned back almost in a swoon, his lips tightly pressed. Now, at the pungent odor of ammonia, he coughed and blinked open his eyes. Before he could utter his protest, however, Beatrice said calmly in a reasonable tone of voice, "I shan't fuss over you, my lord, so no need to frown. But a doctor should look at you—just to make sure that your previous injuries have not become worse and to make sure about the injury to your head. It is only prudent. He fell from the curricle," she explained. "I do not think he sustained a serious injury, but the fall itself must have been quite painful. Do be reasonable, my lord."

The baron's grim features relaxed and he shut his eyes once more. The color returned slowly to his face.

"I do hope nothing is really broken," said Beatrice worriedly to Edgar. "I could not discern any great swelling, but he seems to be in such great pain."

"The injuries he received to his arm and leg cause him pain occasionally; but if only he would refrain from exerting himself too much, he would come to no harm. He should drive with circumspection and not ride at all, let alone in this wild fashion. But there—"

"Edgar," moaned Albinia. "I do not feel well at all. I think I am about to swoon. Where is my vinaigrette? Indeed, I am a much tried creature, and why I have not sunk into a decline is something I cannot fathom."

I can, thought Beatrice with wry amusement.

An interruption occurred in the person of Pedmore, bearing a tray with glasses, decanters of brandy and ratafia, and a plate of cakes. After the glasses were filled and the butler removed himself, the gentlemen and Beatrice picked up their glasses, but Albinia, shaking her head, said in a plaintive tone, "I think I shall seek my bed now. I don't wish this ratafia. I shall have some tea in my chamber. Oh, and if Dr. Maynard is sent for yet tonight, desire him to come to my chamber." She pressed a hand to her thin bosom. "I doubt I shall repose myself without laudanum tonight."

She stared at Beatrice with resentment. "Grandfather and his singular ill-conceived will. Of course he did not bargain on *such* a turn of events." She cast a malevolent look at her brother. "Brook is the most inconsiderate, selfish man. And so you shall find out before you are much older." She dabbed at her eyes with a wisp of a handkerchief. "Edgar, your arm."

Edgar, still holding his glass of wine, hesitated.

"Edgar!" cried Albinia sharply, then moaned and stumbled to her feet.

The baron, who had picked up his glass and was sipping it slowly, looked on the scene with sardonic amusement.

Beatrice took a sip of ratafia and bit into a cake, savoring its sweet smooth texture. In spite of all, she was hungry.

"I shall desire Pedmore to fetch some tea, with our good Devon cream, to your chamber," the baron said to Beatrice, studying her thoughtfully. No fear of her having hysterics, he concluded with satisfaction. She had acquitted herself admirably today. "Something to eat too. Would a light repast be enough, or would you prefer—?"

"That would be sufficient," said Beatrice, pleasantly struck by his consideration. After what Albinia had just said . . .

Edgar was reluctantly supporting Albinia to the door. "I trust you shall have a restful sleep after such an over-setting day, Aunt Beatrice. Aunt?" he abruptly exclaimed. "You could be my sister. I beg your pardon, but . . . but you look so youthful."

"Trying to turn her up sweet already," said Lord Brook with a sardonic curl to his lip.

Beatrice cast a cold glance at her husband. Why was he so out-of-reason cross with his nephew? He ought to be grateful that Edgar treated his wife a trifle better than his precious sister did.

Her lips curved in an inviting smile. "Pray call me Beatrice, if it makes you more comfortable," she said warmly to Edgar.

"I shall be honored," he responded, and went off with his aunt.

Beatrice and Lord Brook remained alone. The baron had placed his glass on the side table and was staring ahead of him with unseeing eyes. He countenance seemed very pensive and sad. It was obvious that his mind was far away.

Beatrice hesitated to break in on his reverie, but as the silence became too uncomfortable, she said slowly, "Are you feeling a trifle better, my lord?"

"Hmm?" He looked up. "I beg your pardon. I did not attend."

"Your arm, your head . . . "

"Oh." He waved his injuries away as unimportant, even as he winced. Sighing deeply, he rose to his feet. He stared at her long and hard, and kept staring—in a way that she suddenly found disconcerting. And felt herself growing hot.

"You are very beautiful, you know," he said softly. Abruptly his countenance hardened. He shook his head impatiently. What was he about? he thought with self-disgust. He was finished with all that. Finished. "I am obliged to leave Brook Manor tomorrow," he said in a cold tone. "And this time you cannot come with me," he added harshly.

"Leaving again, so soon?" Beatrice cried out in dismay. "But your injuries."

"Dr. Maynard will take a look at them. And I shant' ride or drive myself."

"But where do you have to go now? Is it something else to do with your inheritance?"

Resentment flared in his dark eyes. "I am not obliged to give you an account of my comings and goings," he snapped. "My business affairs are solely my own concern."

Beatrice bit her lip. "To be sure. After all, I am your wife in name only," she said bitterly. "But," she added with spirit, "I am persuaded our bargain included your making certain I would at least feel comfortable in your home while you are away."

He frowned. "Now, who would be making you uncomfortable?" he asked. "You must not regard Albinia's megrims and hysterics. She treats us all equally well to her hysterical exhibitions."

"Albinia? No, not so much Albinia. She vexes me, but her conduct toward me is excusable. She is used to being the mistress of Brook Manor."

He bowed. "Handsome of you to make excuses for her."

"Well, I am not unreasonable. But the domestics, especially Mrs. Teswick, are another matter. They dislike me and resent my presence here." Dislike? Mrs. Teswick hated her. What was worse, she wouldn't carry out some of Beatrice's requests, finding excuses for not doing so and contriving at the same time to make Beatrice appear to be in the wrong.

The baron's mouth tightened. Anger flared up in his dark eyes, but he merely said, "They cannot dislike you, they hardly know you. This is just your overwrought fancy."

"I am not overwrought. And they *do* dislike and resent me. Especially Mrs. Teswick. She cannot abide me."

"You must not refine too much on Mrs. Teswick's display of sensibility."

"Sensibility? Sensibility!" cried Beatrice, much outraged.

"Sensibility," repeated Lord Brook firmly. "You heard Albinia say Teswick regards herself as the virtual mistress of this establishment. With Albinia's indolence and her *indifferent"*—his lips curled with derision—"state of health, it is hardly surprising that Teswick became a trifle autocratic. Naturally your arrival has put her nose out of joint. She ran Brook Manor—very efficiently—for my father." Efficiently? thought a skeptical Beatrice. She had observed dust on the furniture. "But *you* are the mistress of the house, and Teswick is only a housekeeper. You should be able to put her in her place."

Beatrice heaved a sigh. "I don't wish to provoke a crisis."

"My God, surely you can handle the domestics without provoking one. You are not a schoolroom miss. Now, pray don't bother me with domestic trifles. I have more important things on my mind."

Such as? it was on the tip of Beatrice's tongue to say, but she forbore it. "I am known to handle domestics very well indeed," she said coldly, trying to contain her mounting anger.

The baron turned to go, then hesitated, his countenance a battlefield of different emotions. "I . . . I beg your pardon if I have spoken too harshly," he said in an expressionless tone. "I have no cause to berate you." He touched his head and grimaced. "It must be that injury that is making me so out-of-reason cross with you. I apologize."

Beatrice's anger melted on the instant. "Of course." He was not feeling well. Such a fall as he had had would make anyone as cross as crabs. Let alone a man of his disposition. If only he were not obliged to leave again tomorrow.

She took a deep breath. "I accept your apology and I

do understand that you cannot be on your best conduct, in the circumstances." He had conducted himself civilly enough most of the time. He had not wished her to come along with him, but he had given in with reasonable grace. And allowed her to accompany him while he inspected the premises and the grounds. "And of course I shall contrive quite well in your absence. But I still wish you were not obliged to go. Pray be careful, Gareth."

Something like a faint hint of a smile touched his lips and eyes. "That's better," he said approvingly. "I was beginning to think you disliked the sound of my name. You have been so studiously avoiding using it up to now."

"Oh, no, not at all. It's just . . . I'm not used to calling you by your first name."

"You do it very well. I dislike formality. Formality and pomp," he said abruptly in a harsh voice with a vehemence that startled Beatrice. The smile had vanished from his face, leaving it grim and set. Suppressed rage glittered in his eyes. "Formality, graciousness, and politeness . . . and underneath, hypocrisy, treachery, and deceit. I prefer the plain honest countryman who speaks his mind openly and finds faults with you to your face."

A frown creased Beatrice's brow. What was he alluding to? "I'm not above mincing matters myself," she said in a puzzled voice, "but one does not have to be rude to be honest."

He glanced at her with an arrested look. "You are in the right of it, Beatrice," he said, "but sometimes I cannot help being rude."

He approached closer, raising his arm as if to touch her. Then he let it fall and bowed stiffly, formally. "I must seek my bed now."

"Shall I see you at breakfast?" Beatrice asked.

"Perhaps. I might be obliged to call on some of my

tenants at their cottages on the moor. If I do, I shall breakfast at home. I trust you shall be able to sleep well, even after such a harrowing experience. Oh, in case I haven't said so, my thanks to you for what you did today. And my apologies for the incident." The color mounted to his face and his dark eyes looked troubled. "You *could* have been killed. I shall give you a word of warning: don't ever drive with me, Beatrice, when I am handling the ribbons."

"But must you drive in this breakneck fashion?" she asked.

His lips twisted in a bitter line. "I must, if the devil drives," he said harshly.

A baffling answer. "Will you be away long?"

"I am not sure. A few days, perhaps. Good night, Beatrice." And he turned on his heel and walked out, stiff and erect. And though he dragged his foot a little, he did not stumble or relax his ramrod stance.

Beatrice looked at his retreating back with mixed feelings. Her new husband was a difficult man to fathom, but she would be sorry to see him leave on the morrow. And not so much because she would be obliged to fend for herself without his support. After all, she told herself, nothing could possibly arise during his brief absence that she couldn't cope with.

She couldn't have been more mistaken.

Four

Beatrice stirred drowsily on the bed, then blinked open her eyes. She stared about her, at first without comprehension; then, becoming quite awake, she realized. Of course. She was back in her room at Brook Manor. The sun streaming through the open window brightened the gloomy dark oak furniture and the wainscoting, and the fresh breeze billowed the green velvet curtains. Beatrice fancied the sweet tangy scent of the moor carried on the air.

She gazed at the bright oblong of the window, but in her mind's eye she saw the tall striking figure of her husband. Before the wedding, he had been but the means of saving her family from ruin and a preferable alternative to the old gouty squire. But now, only a few days into their marriage, she could not feel so dispassionately about him anymore. Some of his conduct filled her with misgivings and puzzled her, but she could not help appreciating his good qualities, his skill at the ribbons— even though it verged on foolhardiness—and the strong masculinity that emanated from his lean, hard-muscled body. She hoped the injuries he had sustained in the fall would prove as slight as he believed them to be, and trusted his doctor would not allow him to embark on a journey if he were in no condition to do so.

Abruptly she sat bolt upright in bed. It must be past breakfasttime, it finally dawned on her. Breakfast, taken in the family dining room, was an informal affair, with the family members often repairing for breakfast at different times; but Beatrice did not wish to miss her husband if he had decided to breakfast at home.

She dressed hastily but with care in a simple but becoming dress of rose silk, her shiny black hair piled on top of her head and confined by a rose velvet ribbon, with one long curl allowed to fall forward on one side.

As she crossed the great hall in the direction of the dining room, she again observed how gloomy the hall appeared when not ablaze with candles. Daylight streaming through the windows was hardly adequate to disperse the gloom. In contrast, the family dining room was a bright cheery place remodeled by Adam and decorated in green and gold. All the windows were tall, reaching almost to the floor.

Beatrice's heartbeat quickened as she placed her hand on the doorknob. Would her husband be breakfasting there?

He was. Sitting at the head of the large mahogany table. A footman in green-and-gold livery hovered above him, ready to supply more food from the handsome mahogany sideboard. Albinia, dressed in a blue-gray silk gown and a fetching blue cap, a gray silver-fringed shawl over her shoulders, was sitting at his right side. Edgar was just in the process of sitting down.

Beatrice knew how strongly the baron's sister resented giving up her seat at the foot of the table. "Good morning," she said in a calm voice that belied her inner apprehension.

The baron looked up. He did not look well. His countenance was pale and his eyes were red-rimmed, as if from lack of sleep. But he was impeccably attired in breeches and a maroon coat of excellent cut. "Good morning, Beatrice," he said in an indifferent voice. "I trust you had a good night."

"I did. Thank you, my lord."

"Indeed, one can see that at a glance. You look ravishing," said Edgar enthusiastically, his eyes crinkling in appreciation. "Good morning, Beatrice."

The baron scowled, while Albinia gave Beatrice an ungracious nod.

"Has the doctor attended you, my lord?" Beatrice asked her husband with concern.

He nodded. "Yes. You may rest easy. My injuries are but trifling ones."

"Thank God for that." But they must have given him pain during the night.

"We were persuaded you would sleep until noon," Albinia said to Beatrice in a petulant voice, as if resenting her appearance at the table.

"I am an early riser as a rule," said Beatrice, suppressing the stirrings of anger within her as she took her seat at the table.

The footman served food from the sideboard, and for a while silence reigned in the dining room, made somewhat less uncomfortable because of the diners' preoccupation with their meal. Edgar, however, did not allow the silence to stretch too long, engaging Beatrice in lighthearted conversation, while Albinia, picking at her food, complained about the shortcomings of the servants and the indifferent state of her health. The baron contributed to the conversation with monosyllables.

Beatrice was halfway through her meal when he pushed back his chair and rose. "I must leave now."

"Will you be back for dinner before you set out on your journey?" asked Beatrice.

He shook his head. "I shall dine at the posting inn on the way. I—"

Loud, excited barking from the courtyard interrupted him. All eyes instantly turned toward the open window. There, with his tawny head upon the low sill, was the most beautiful collie Beatrice had ever seen.

"It's Prince," cried Edgar. "He belongs to Squire Cavanaugh, our nearest neighbor."

Albinia shuddered. "I wish you would discourage the squire, Brook. I find his intrusion into our life most vexing."

"You know very well it is impossible to discourage Roger," he answered, frowning. He lowered his voice. "A word of warning, Beatrice. Don't tell the squire anything you don't wish spread all over the countryside within an hour. He is an inveterate gossip."

"Down, Prince, down," a hearty voice boomed, and then a man appeared at the window. He stepped carefully over the windowsill into the chamber.

The middle-aged man looked indeed like a country squire, Beatrice observed. Round countenance, ruddy complexion, blond gray-peppered mustache, and sparse blond-and-gray hair, she noticed when he took off his hat and threw it carelessly at the footman. He was dressed in serviceable boots and breeches and a brown coat.

" 'Morning, everybody," he said in a loud, genial voice. "Don't rise and don't interrupt your breakfast." He waved his hand at them. "You know I stand on no ceremony with you." As yet he had not noticed Beatrice. "I'm sure you won't mind, Brook, if I partake of breakfast with you. I set out quite early this morning."

Lord Brook, with a resigned expression on his countenance, reseated himself.

The squire turned around and his eyes alighted on Beatrice. He swept her a deep bow. "Your bride, I collect?"

"Squire Roger Cavanaugh . . . my wife, Beatrice," Lord Brook performed the introductions.

The squire came forward, exuding a faint aroma of the stables. "Delighted to make your acquaintance, Lady Brook," he said as he bowed over her hand. "You don't mind a guest for breakfast, do you, ma'am?"

"No, of course not. Pray take a seat."

The footman stepped forward, but the squire waved him away. "No, no, I shall help myself, Murphy, much obliged."

The footman hesitated, pleased because the squire recalled his name, yet wishful to perform his duty. But the squire helped himself liberally to some cold beef and slices of ham from the sideboard and carried the heaping plate to the table. "Always believe in a hearty breakfast. You should eat more, Albinia," he said, plunking his plate next to hers on the table.

Albinia shuddered, wrinkling her nose, and pressed a fine cambric handkerchief delicately to her nostrils. "You could have at least changed before paying us a call," she said in a plaintive voice.

The squire's blue-green eyes widened innocently. "Why? You know I stand on no ceremony with you."

"Oh, you are impossible!" cried Albinia, very much vexed. He was either impervious to her snub or blissfully unaware of the meaning behind her words.

"I hope you shall like it here, Lady Brook," said the squire, cocking his head to one side as he speared a large piece of beef on his fork. "People either love the moor or hate it. Nothing in between. Me, I'd liefer reside her than any other place on earth. Albinia, now,"—he waved with the fork—"she likes it here right enough. Trouble is, she hardly ever sets foot on the heather now."

"You don't expect *me* to tramp in bogs, in mud up to my knees. I would ruin my clothes. Not to mention my constitution, which, as you well know, is very delicate."

The squire popped the meat into his mouth, chewed it, swallowed, and waving the empty fork at her, said, "Would do you good if you went tramping about a bit like I do."

Albinia shuddered. "Never! I could never trust

myself out there. Why, I might fall into a bog, and all you could see of me would be the hat, like that poor man. Oh, it was dreadful."

"You weren't so afraid of the moor . . . once," said the squire, cocking his head at her and regarding her quizzically.

"What happened, ma'am?" asked Beatrice, interested.

"A rider on his horse rode into the bog and it swallowed them whole. Only the man's hat was visible above the morass."

"Nonsense," snapped the baron. "It's not true, of course."

"Have people drowned in the bog there?" asked Beatrice.

"Indeed they have," said Edgar, who up to now had been silent, his friendly, handsome countenance creased in annoyance. Clearly, as Albinia, he did not welcome the squire's call. "There are many dangerous places on the moor. But in general, during daylight it is perfectly safe to venture there."

"Daylight or nighttime, I would never dare venture out there," said Albinia. "What of the farmer who disappeared into Fox Tor Mire, or that peddler who got lost on Cranmere and was never seen again?"

"Is that true, Squire Cavanaugh?" asked Beatrice. "Did these people meet their end in the bog?"

The squire rubbed his nose pensively. "We cannot be sure about those two. But people *have* disappeared on the moor right enough. No question but some places are dangerous, and cattle die there all the time. Especially at this time, in the spring. But many mires and bogs that would not support an animal would support a man stepping with care. Important thing to remember is, when *stogged,* keep going on at any cost, so there's no time to sink in very deeply. And don't panic and thrash about when you land in a *stable.* Cattle thrash about, and ponies, and as soon as they start doing that, they're done for.''

"And do you venture into those dangerous places?" asked Beatrice.

"Oh, I go everywhere. I know this place well, and so does Prince, my dog. I'll be taking a walk on the moor right now. Care to accompany me, Brook?"

"No, I am obliged to leave Brook Manor for a few days. But I shall be calling on some of my tenants first, so I must make haste." He rose. "Pray excuse me."

"I shall see you to the door, m'boy," said the squire.

"But you haven't finished eating."

"The food won't run away. Don't remove it, Murphy."

A loud bark made them turn to the window. The collie had his paws on the windowsill, his head cocked, as his master's had been before.

"I shan't leave you behind. I shall be back in a trice," said the squire, pushing back his chair and rising.

Two things then happened at once. The dog bounded over the sill and jumped into the room, while the dining-room door opened to reveal Pedmore, who announced, "Miss Camilla Swinton."

Five

The dog bounded forward, barking excitedly.

Albinia shrank back, upsetting her teacup and spilling tea on her dress and on the table, and cried out in horror. Murphy, the footman, rushed forward to mop up the spill, while the newcomer bent down to pat the dog's head. "Naughty Prince," she said. "You mustn't let him come into the room, squire. Good morning, Albinia, Edgar. I thought I would pay a call on you, Albinia. I was not aware Gareth had returned." Her brows rose in a questioning look at Beatrice. "Good morning, Gareth, squire."

The baron gave the newcomer a curt nod. Beatrice rose to her feet. "Camilla Swinton . . . my wife, Beatrice," the baron said coldly, his face an expressionless mask, except for his eyes, which burned with some suppressed emotion.

"My congratulations," said Camilla in a voice difficult to fathom. "Welcome to our little close-knit circle. I hope you shall fit in well."

Albinia, still dabbing ineffectively at her dress, said to Beatrice, "Camilla is our neighbor and my closest friend. I do hope you two shall become friends also." But the tone of her voice indicated that she doubted it very much. "Roger, pray take away this beast at once," she added, as the dog kept circling around their legs and barking intermittently.

Beatrice bent down to pat the dog's tawny head, taking pleasure in the soft feeling of his silky fur. She thought the animal was delightful. The dog nuzzled her palm and waved his tail in a friendly manner.

"That's unusual. He doesn't take easily to strangers," remarked the squire, glancing with approbation at Beatrice. "Out, Prince," he commanded. "You are offending Albinia's sensibilities."

"At least *he* doesn't smell like his master," said Albinia *sotto voce,* but Beatrice felt sure the squire must have heard it. He gave no indication that he did, but began to move toward the door, the dog following him. Edgar, however, did hear it, and though he did not welcome the squire's call, he seemed scandalized by Albinia's words.

"Aunt, pray don't," he begged in a low voice, earning a darkling look from Albinia.

"Pray take a seat, Miss Swinton," said Beatrice, reseating herself.

Camilla sat down at the table, but declined any breakfast. The two young women regarded each other.

Beatrice saw a tall woman in her twenties with chestnut hair, dark eyes, and a complexion tanned by the sun. Her figure was good, but one could see at a glance she was more used to riding than to the drawing room, even if she smelled of violets and not the stables. She was attired in a green riding dress of simple but excellent cut, strong boots, and a green velvet hat. Beatrice could see nothing objectionable about her, yet for some reason she took her in instant dislike.

"Camilla is an excellent rider," said Albinia with pride. "And the best rider to hounds, barring the squire."

"Indeed yes," corroborated Edgar warmly. "She is a bruising rider. Quite cast me in the shade with her prowess at taking hurdles."

"No need to be modest, m'boy," said the squire. "You're as good as they come—*in the daylight.*"

Edgar reddened and bit his lip. And Beatrice had to revise her opinion of the squire, though she had liked him very much at the outset. But must he embarrass poor Edgar with his fear of darkness? Still, to a man of the squire's stamp, such fear would be quite incomprehensible.

"Pray excuse me, ladies, Edgar," said Lord Brook, and strode through the door, followed by the squire. The dog, waving his tail, trotted after them. It was all very informal, yet Beatrice definitely sensed a tension in the air.

Her husband's treatment of Camilla seemed cold and distant—hardly the proper attitude to a close family friend. Camilla's attitude toward him seemed casual and indifferent. But was it? The dark eyes seemed to measure Beatrice in a calculating way. Did she fancy it, or was there hostility lurking in them? Beatrice gave an inward sigh. Why not? Everyone else was hostile toward her.

Camilla glanced back as the doors were closing behind the baron, the squire, and the dog. Beatrice fancied she saw hatred flare up for an instant in her dark eyes. The expression was so fleeting, however, that she could have just imagined it.

Albinia fanned herself. "Thank heaven he has gone for the moment," she said of the squire. "A dreadful man, reeking of stables and coming here at all hours of the day, not at all caring whether it is convenient for me . . . us to receive him. And can you conceive his insensibility and impropriety? He stays here for as long as it pleases him. No amount of hinting or snubs will put him out of countenance or make him realize that he is not welcome. Short of ordering him out—unthinkable —there is no way of getting rid of him. An impossible man."

"I think Squire Cavanaugh realizes more than we give him credit for," said Camilla.

"Nonsense," said Albinia. "He is just an old fool." But Beatrice was inclined to be of Camilla's opinion.

"Do you ride, Lady Brook?" Camilla asked in a polite way, but Beatrice fancied again a hidden hostility.

And why not? Camilla was a neighbor and a friend of the family, and the baron was a very eligible man. Yet he had chosen to marry a stranger. It was not to be wondered at if Camilla regarded Beatrice with resentment. "Yes, I do ride," she answered. "My groom shall be here with my horse tomorrow. I do hope so, for I haven't ridden in days, what with the wedding and all."

Camilla nodded sympathetically. "I understand perfectly. I cannot feel alive when I am not riding across the moor."

"But aren't you afraid of landing in the bog?"

Camilla looked at her scornfully. "I am not afraid, for I've roamed here all my life. Of course, I wouldn't advise *you* to ride there. Riding on the moor is quite a different matter from cantering sedately in Hyde Park, which is about the extent of riding you city-bred ladies are accustomed to."

Her tone was so supercilious and condescending, Beatrice could have slapped her insolent countenance. So Camilla thought her good only for riding in the park. Beatrice ground her teeth. Well, she would prove that she was just as good a rider as Camilla. If not better.

"It is a pity I don't have my mount here, or I would go riding yet today," she said, not attempting to defend her riding skills. That would have been beneath her dignity.

"I would be most happy to place my mount at your disposal," said Edgar.

"But Gareth has an excellent stable," said Camilla. "I am certain he would be pleased to let you ride one of his horses, or even his own Fencer, if he is not riding him."

"No, not Fencer," said Edgar quickly. "But this is an excellent suggestion."

"You're right. Fencer would never do," said Camilla. "He is much too spirited an animal. I'm afraid females, especially those bred in the city, could never mount him. Only *I* can ride Fencer," she added with pride.

Oh, is *that* so? thought Beatrice, gritting her teeth. Then and there she decided she would ride her husband's horse. Her instant dislike of Camilla must have been intuitive. That toplofty woman had to be shown that no longer would *she* be the only riding queen of the moor.

"I'm afraid it is only too true," Edgar corroborated. "Camilla is quite intrepid. Even I would never dare place myself on Fencer's back."

Beatrice's eyes sparkled with challenge. "*I* would. Care to wager on it, Edgar? And you, Miss Swinton?"

Camilla gave her her superior smile. "I never wager on a certainty, Lady Brook. You would lose the wager."

Anger flashed in Beatrice's deep blue eyes. "Well, Edgar? Do you also think that I cannot contrive to put Fencer through his paces?"

"I'm sure you are an excellent rider, Beatrice. But never having seen you on a horse, I cannot tell for certain."

"But would you wager on it?" she persisted.

"Ha, what would he wager with?" Albinia snorted. Apparently Edgar was not left well-provided-for by his parents, Beatrice thought. "Oh no," Albinia moaned, "there he is again with that dreadful dog."

And indeed the squire had returned to the dining room, the dog trotting ahead of him, wagging his tail. "For heaven's sake, Roger, get that beast out of here," said Albinia, goaded beyond endurance. "You know I detest dogs. You bring him along just to torment me."

"*I* torment *you*? Now, Albinia, you know in what esteem I hold you," he said with a roguish twinkle in his eye. And to Beatrice's astonishment, Albinia actually blushed.

"That's what you always say, but you are completely insensitive to my wishes."

"I collect you are quite a friend of the family, Squire Cavanaugh," said Beatrice.

Albinia laughed. "*Friend,* I wouldn't know. But he has run tame at Brook Manor ever since he was in short coats. A favorite with both my grandfathers. I cannot conceive why," she added, pouting.

"It's too bad you are not riding today, squire, or I would accompany you," said Beatrice. "I have a fancy to go riding on the moor now, but my mount won't be here until tomorrow. Do you think I could ride Fencer?"

The jovial expression was wiped off the round face. The squire shook his head. "Don't know if you could handle him, but I wouldn't advise you to try. Why not choose some other horse from the stables? I don't think Brook would wish you to take his horse—I doubt he would allow it."

Oh ho, so he wouldn't, thought Beatrice with indignation. But he would allow *her.*

"I beg you, forget all about this notion of riding Fencer," said Edgar earnestly. "Or at least beg leave of Brook first. Best wait until your own mount arrives. I'm sure there are many things you would wish to do. Become better acquainted with Brook Manor, for instance. I would be most happy to show you around the estate."

"You forget, Edgar, that you have promised to call on Oliver after breakfast," said Camilla, her honeyed tone and expression imperfectly masking the sharp edge of her voice.

Edgar's face fell. "To be sure. I had forgotten.

Perhaps I can show you around when I get back.''

"Mrs. Teswick can perform that duty admirably," said Camilla. "Or would you?" She glanced at Albinia.

Albinia waved at her with her fan. "Not I. Tramping all over the place would be far too exhausting for me. Best wait for Brook to do so, Beatrice."

The squire, who had reseated himself and begun again to eat, was regarding the group about him with kind yet—Beatrice suddenly realized—quite shrewd eyes.

The dog had trotted over to Beatrice, and she was absently fondling his satiny ear.

Abruptly the squire laid down his knife and fork. "Forgot something to ask of Brook. Murphy, go and discover if your master is still around."

Murphy went, but returned immediately. "He's just left, sir."

"Humph. Well, you had better clear my plate, boy. I'd better be leaving." He grinned wickedly at Albinia. "That ought to make you happy. But I shall be back."

"I would never doubt that," said Albinia sourly.

The squire gave a graceful bow to the assembled company. "Good day to you all. Pleased to have made your acquaintance, Lady Brook. If there is anything you need, or if you find yourself in a hobble, please call on me anytime." Just as Beatrice was to thank him, warming to him again, he said to Edgar, "Don't stay out after dark, m'boy." It was cruel to remind Edgar of his fear thus constantly, thought Beatrice. It was obvious the squire disliked Edgar. Why?

"Come, Prince. By your leave, Lady Brook, Albinia, we shall take the shortcut again." As the squire headed for the window, the dog, who had flopped on the floor beside Beatrice, jumped to his feet and bounded over to the window ahead of him.

When the two had gone—the squire had turned back after he had crossed the sill and waved a cheery arm—

Albinia fell back in her chair with a moan. "Thank God he is gone. Murphy, ascertain if the carpet is wet. Have it cleaned instantly."

"Yes, ma'am."

Albinia tottered to her feet. "I am sorry, Camilla, but I must rest. The squire's call leaves me quite exhausted. Edgar, your arm."

Edgar hesitated, as if wishing to say something to Beatrice, but Albinia repeated a peremptory "Edgar!"

He sighed and spread his hands apologetically. "Perhaps you could take a turn in the garden, Beatrice. Or walk in the park. Camilla would be glad to accompany you."

But Camilla was not inclined to do so. "Pray excuse me, Lady Brook, but I am not one to walk sedately in a garden or a park. I am far too restless for that, too energetic. Besides, I only came to pay a call on Albinia."

"I am surprised that you two are such good friends, you are so different."

"But we have known each other since childhood. I spent as much time at Brook Manor as at Swinton Court. Our families were very close. Alas, there are only two of us now, I and my brother Oliver. Sir Oliver," she added. "And pray don't take amiss my warning—stay away from Fencer. Of all things Brook hates most is to have a stranger touch his mount. Oh, I beg your pardon. Of course you are not a stranger, but you *are* a stranger to Fencer. And believe me, he is far too high-spirited for you. There is a fine old chestnut mare in the stables, Cherryred. She would do perfectly for you."

Beatrice's eyes blazed with wrath. She had to bite her tongue not to give this creature a well deserved set-down. "Don't be so sure about me, Miss Swinton. As they say, don't wager on an unknown horse. *You* have never seen me mounted."

"True, true. But you are a city-bred female. And—"

"And I have ridden since I was six years old. And I resent the patronizing tone you take with me," Beatrice burst out. "Oh, I know I am not one of the moor people. Apparently I don't belong. But that is no reason to suppose that any female born outside of Dartmoor is a dim-witted pea-goose. I assure you that I am not."

The dark eyes glittered with venom. "You are nothing if not honest, Lady Brook. But you misunderstood my motives. I have merely been trying to make things easier for Gareth. I know him so well, you see."

"Then I wonder you didn't marry him," snapped Beatrice.

If looks could kill, Beatrice would have been dead on the instant. The deadly expression, however, lasted only about a second. Then it became veiled by lowered lids, and when next Camilla lifted her eyes, all expression was wiped off them, except cold indifference. "Brook is a difficult man to get along with," she said in an expressionless tone. "And I am not one to bow easily to autocratic whims."

Neither am I, thought Beatrice, much incensed but also vexed with herself for having lost her temper.

She took a deep breath. "Pray forgive my heated speech," she forced herself to say against her will. "I collect we just misunderstood each other. When we are better acquainted, and I hope we shall be, then we both shall shed our prejudices and see each other in a clearer light." She almost choked on the words, but she got them out. It wouldn't do to openly antagonize someone held in such high esteem by all, and a friend of the family to boot. She made a great effort to crease her countenance into a false smile. "Cry friends, Miss Swinton?" she said, and extended her hand.

Camilla's brows lifted. "You are full of surprises, Lady Brook," she said quizzically, but took the proffered hand. "Cry friends," she said, creasing her countenance into just as sincere a smile as Beatrice's. "I shall take my leave of you now," she said, rising, "and I trust I shall see you in good health when I meet you next. Good day. Oh, and pray call me Camilla."

"And you may call me Beatrice," said Beatrice, swallowing her revulsion. She rose also, reaching for the bell pull, but Camilla said, "Pray don't trouble yourself. I shall show myself out. I know the way well."

"I'm sure you do," said Beatrice with a grimace of distaste.

After Camilla had gone, Beatrice reseated herself and remained at the table for a while, thinking. In spite of her determination to ride Fencer, she had some misgivings about taking the horse. She decided to let her temper cool before attempting the ride.

Meanwhile, she would like to be shown around the house. She rang the bell for Mrs. Teswick, and when the housekeeper stood in front of her, arms crossed, the gray eyes regarding her with hostility, Beatrice said in a calm voice she was far from feeling, "Mrs. Teswick, I should like to become better acquainted with the manor. Pray conduct me through the chambers."

The hostile stare intensified. "Now?"

"Of course, now," Beatrice said, irritated.

The housekeeper's lips pressed into an uncompromising line. "I cannot do so, madam. I have my duties to perform."

Beatrice controlled her temper with difficulty. "Surely they can wait for half an hour," she said in what she hoped was a reasonable tone, with just a touch of haughtiness.

"It would take more than half an hour, madam."

"Well, desire Pedmore to conduct me, then."

"Pedmore takes his orders only from his lordship or Miss Risborough."

Beatrice blinked. Surely not. This was just another of Mrs. Teswick's attempts to vex her. "Pray do not tell me that you cannot command a footman or a maid," she countered. "It makes no difference who conducts me, as long as it is someone well acquainted with the house. Or can none of *them* be spared either?"

The housekeepers's face remained stonily hostile and stubborn. "The servants are all engaged upon their tasks. They cannot just leave everything on the instant. Unless your ladyship fancies to go without dinner or have the chambers left unswept—and the silver not polished. Should the underfootman leave off polishing the silver when he has just spread the polishing paste on the plate, or should—"

Beatrice put up a hand. This was deliberate provocation. The housekeeper was hoping perhaps to present the baron with a domestic crisis upon his return. Why? Why was she so hostile to her? Beatrice could insist, of course, on being obeyed—as she had every right. She could even threaten the housekeeper, but she did not wish to—so soon upon becoming the Lady of the Manor. So no one could be spared, she thought scornfully. With fifty servants at Brook Manor, several, let alone one, *could* be spared at a moment's notice. She could just ring for one of them, or for Pedmore, after dismissing the housekeeper. But suddenly she had lost her wish to look over the premises.

She took a deep breath, trying to control her rising temper. "I'm sure someone *could* be spared at this moment," she said coldly. "But I shan't dispute that fact now. I shall talk to you about this later. You may go."

After the housekeeper had gone, Beatrice discovered that she was shaking and bathed in perspiration. Had she done the right thing? she wondered. She should have forced the issue, she fumed. But she wished to avoid hostile confrontation as much as possible. She had no desire to disrupt the Brook household.

Beatrice went slowly up to her chamber to change. She *would* ride Fencer at once.

Gareth might be vexed at her taking the horse without his leave, but if the animal came to no harm, he would have no cause to upbraid her.

She would take no groom with her. She wished to be alone. The moor was not a London park, but Beatrice had ridden and walked in the country alone before.

And she would take just a short ride on the moor. The sun was shining, all was calm, and she would not venture too far out. Surely nothing untoward could occur, she reasoned—if she were careful. After all, if Camilla and the squire could roam all over the moors, so could she.

Six

By the time Beatrice changed into her blue velvet riding dress with gold epaulets à la Hussar, and a fetching blue hat with an ostrich plume, she was somewhat more composed. And even hungry.

Abruptly she realized that she hadn't finished her breakfast. Should she ring to have something sent up? she debated. No. On her way out, she would go to the kitchen for some bread and butter to take along on the moor.

Holding up the skirts of her riding dress, she went down to the great hall and asked a passing footman for directions to the kitchen.

His eyes widened at her words. "But . . . but Miss Albinia never goes near the kitchen," he stammered.

"Well, I do. So pray tell me where it is."

The footman, quite astounded, led Beatrice through a maze of passages to the west wing and the servants' quarters. As they were nearing the kitchen, raised voices could be heard. Suddenly a piercing wail assailed their ears.

The footman glanced around nervously. "May I leave now, your ladyship?" Clearly he wished to escape.

Beatrice increased her pace. "What is going forward there? Is it coming from the kitchen?"

"Yes, ma'am. That chamber to the right. Pray, ma'am, may I go? I don't wish for no trouble."

"Why should *you* be in trouble? What is happening there? Do you know?" she added sharply as loud sobbing now could be heard from the kitchen. And a crash, as if a pan or a pot had fallen to the floor. Another voice, a male one, was now raised in protest, followed by a barrage of French words.

"I don't know nothing, ma'am," said the footman. "But when Teswick and Gaston are at outs, it is wise not to step in between them."

"Who is Gaston?"

"The chef. He is French. Pray, ma'am, may I go?" They were by the kitchen door.

"Oh, very well," said Beatrice crossly. But this was beyond all bounds that the whole household should be terrified of Mrs. Teswick. She opened the kitchen door.

This lofty chamber presented a strange appearance.

Two kitchen maids cowered in a corner of the room. By the big hearth stood a middle-aged man in a chef's tall hat, wringing his hands and jabbering away in French. And in the middle of the floor stood the housekeeper, stiff and unyielding, her finger pointing accusingly at a young kitchen maid cringing beside the table. On the floor, beside two upturned pans, was a mess of broken eggs, yolks and whites oozing over the floor, snaking up to the housekeeper's shiny black shoes. Some of the eggs, on being broken, had splashed onto the kitchen maid's white apron.

"Oh, pray . . . oh, pray, don't turn me off," wailed the girl, folding her hands in supplication.

And Mrs. Teswick was saying, "I have warned you twice before. I shan't warn you again. I don't wish to see you here tomorrow."

"No. Oh, no. I have nowhere to go. I can't go home. I—"

"What is going forward?" asked Beatrice sharply.

Mrs. Teswick whirled around. The chef broke off his tirade, his mouth remaining open in astonishment. And the crouching girl on the floor, sensing a possible reprieve, hurtled herself toward Beatrice. "Oh, my lady . . . oh, pray, say I shan't be turned off," she begged, embracing Beatrice and in the process smearing egg yolk over her riding boots.

Beatrice placed a restraining hand on her shoulder. "Steady, there. Pray calm yourself. What is the meaning of this, Mrs. Teswick? Why should this child be turned off?"

The housekeeper gave Beatrice a hostile stare. "Pray let *me* handle this, madam. This is a domestic matter."

"And I am the mistress of the house," snapped Beatrice. "I repeat, why is she to be turned off?"

"She breaks things. She drops them. She is an imbecile," offered the chef. "But turn her off—ah *non, non.* Set her to work in the chambers. In the sewing room."

"Yes, yes, anywhere. Only don't turn me off," the child implored Beatrice.

"Mrs. Teswick," said Beatrice, "don't turn her off. Give her other duties to perform. Some that she is more suited for."

The housekeeper compressed her lips in disapproval. "She must be punished."

"But not by being turned off. Deduct the price of breakage and eggs from her wages."

"I shall punish her as I see fit," said Mrs. Teswick, folding her arms and staring boldly at Beatrice, as if daring her to countermand her orders.

Something snapped with Beatrice. "Oh, no you shan't," she said, stamping her foot. Or at least she would have stamped it, were it not clutched by the kitchen maid's hands.

The housekeeper drew herself up, affronted. "I take my orders—"

"From *me.* I could tolerate everything for the sake of peace, even your trying to put me out of countenance. But I shan't tolerate your destroying this poor child."

"She is a lazy good-for-nothing and a thief."

"No, no, I didn't steal the cake," cried the girl.

"A cake! A cake? You may steal all the cakes you wish," said Beatrice. "I suppose you would put her in the stocks or have her transported for stealing a piece of cake."

"She must be turned off," the housekeeper repeated stubbornly, two red spots burning on her cheeks, her eyes glittering with rage.

"Take care, Mrs. Teswick, that I shall not turn *you* off, the moment Lord Brook returns and I apprise him of the situation."

"His lordship would never allow *that,*" said Mrs. Teswick triumphantly.

"That remains to be seen. Pray recollect, you—all of you—know nothing of what I'm capable of. Even of bringing Lord Brook round to my thinking." (She didn't think he would dismiss Mrs. Teswick, but no harm in frightening her a little.) "The girl stays."

"I say she shall be turned off," said Mrs. Teswick, taking a step forward, her eyes burning with murderous hate.

Beatrice stood her ground. "Take care what you are about, Mrs. Teswick," she said in a silkily cold voice of lowered tone. "What shall you do if I take this child by the hand now and wish to take her with me? Shall you snatch her away from my hand? Shall you struggle with me? You, a mere housekeeper, and I, the lady of the manor?" That's putting her in her place, Beatrice thought with great satisfaction. "Think of the proprieties, think of the scandal were you to do something so improper. I have no wish to intrude into your running of the house, but you are fast making me change my mind. I shan't tolerate insubordination in a domestic."

The housekeeper looked daggers at Beatrice, and her mouth was still stubbornly set. "I take my orders from Lord Brook," she said.

"You shall take your orders from me—if and when it shall please me to give them. I shan't start doing so, however, for I wish to become better acquainted with everything and everyone. Perhaps if you don't vex me, I shan't intrude into your running of the household at all. But I shan't allow you to turn this girl off. And I give you warning: *no one* shall be turned off—I repeat, *no one*—without my approval. I can assure you *that* Lord Brook shall agree to."

The housekeeper stood stock-still, her bosom heaving, her cheeks, which were quite red, now deathly pale, her eyes dilated in shock. Her features twisted in malevolence. Never had Beatrice seen such hatred in a person's face. With one exception, she abruptly thought. Camilla and the housekeeper could be twins in their feelings toward her.

"Is it understood? Have I made myself plain enough? The girl stays."

The housekeeper nodded wordlessly.

Suddenly Beatrice discovered that her legs were trembling and her knees felt like blancmange. "Pray leave us now. I wish to speak to this girl and to Gaston."

Gaston looked up. "Madame knows my name."

"A footman told me." She lifted the girl, now sobbing with relief and gasping out her thanks, and led her to a bench by the table, seating her and herself sitting down. She did not look to make sure if the housekeeper had gone, but she could hear her footsteps going toward the door and then she could hear the door close. "What is your name, child?" she asked.

"Jean."

"And how old are you?"

"Fifteen."

"Fifteen. Only fifteen. And what would you like to do?"

"I like sewing, ma'am." The girl hiccuped.

Gaston nodded. "Oui, oui. She mended a hole in my sock, that one. I told Madame Teswick to put her in the sewing room. But . . ." He spread his hands in a Gallic gesture. "Ah, she is a dragon, that one. But she cannot threaten *me*. His lordship had fetched me here, and here I stay. She may not like it, but me—I stay. But she doesn't listen to me. She doesn't like me. I am an *étranger,* a foreigner. I am the Frenchy, the frog. Ah, bah. I do not hold with Bonaparte. I am glad he is vanquished at last. Let him rot at Helena. He killed my master."

Ah! Now Beatrice understood. Gaston must have been rescued from Napoleon.

The girl was sniffling and wiping her tears with her apron, smearing egg all over her face. The two kitchen maids, awed, came forward, their mouths agape, their eyes like saucers.

The chef abruptly recollected himself. "You clean this up," he commanded them, pointing to the egg and dishes on the floor. "My lady, you have egg on you. *Permettez-moi.*" And he set about to remove it. "And you, imbecile, don't touch her with your hands."

"Go and wash, Jean, and tell the mistress of the sewing room that I wish to speak with her later. You wait in your chamber or wherever you sleep."

"In the attic, with them." The girl pointed at the two kitchen maids.

"Well, you take a bath and stay there until I return." The girl looked up in alarm.

"Don't be afraid. I am merely going riding on the moor. And Mrs. Teswick shan't touch a hair on your head now."

"Oh, ma'am," cried the girl, and leaned forward to kiss Beatrice's hands, in the process smearing Beatrice and the chef with egg.

"Imbecile," screamed the chef, and threw up his hands. "Go, go and wash."

The girl rose, staring at Beatrice with worshipful eyes. "If there is anything you wish done, ma'am, anything, I'll do it," she said with fervor.

Beatrice patted her on the head. "Perhaps you shall do me a good turn sometime. And when I see you later, you must tell me all about yourself. Now, go and wash up."

The girl was by the door, when it burst open and Pedmore and a footman entered the chamber. The butler gave a correct cool bow to Beatrice. "I apprehend there is some trouble with Jean," he stated in an expressionless tone.

The girl shrank back in terror. "Milady."

Beatrice took a deep breath. "There is none *now*. Obviously the girl is not suited to kitchen work. I have decided she shall work in the sewing room. Pray be so good as to send the sewing-room mistress to my chamber when I return from my ride. And see to it that Jean gets a bath and that she is not bullied by anybody. And I do mean *anybody*."

Dislike yet dawning respect flitted for an instant across the impassive countenance of the butler. Then he bowed. "Very good, my lady. It shall be as you wish."

He doesn't like me, but at least he is not obsessed with hatred toward me, thought Beatrice. The footman stared at her with truculent hostility, yet with awe. But Gaston beamed approvingly and Jean with worship in her eyes.

Beatrice took a deep breath. So be it. The battle lines were drawn. Teswick seemed to be her sworn enemy. The others, in spite of not liking the housekeeper, would perhaps support her against a stranger. Albinia would not lift a finger on Beatrice's behalf. On whom could she count? On Gaston, Jean, and perhaps the two other kitchen maids. Oh, yes, and Edgar.

And her husband? She pushed the doubt resolutely from her mind.

Rising—she couldn't swallow a morsel now, it would choke her—with a firm stride she went to the door.

Seven

The horse pranced in high mettle as Beatrice rode out of the yard of Brook Manor. The sun was shining out of the blue sky, the cool wind caressed her brow, and Beatrice felt a sense of relief just to be out of the house, away from its hostile atmosphere. The road, a path really, barely passable for vehicles, wound its way up the steep slope of the moor. The horse, a beautiful gray stallion, fresh and frisky, was champing for a gallop, but Beatrice restrained him. She must get her bearings first. At an easy canter she followed the road up.

By daylight the scenery looked a trifle less grim than at night. Patches of new growth were visible; the uniform shadowy ground covering of last night revealed itself as heather, gorse, and some other bushes Beatrice could not identify. She saw as well some emerald-green circles like those she had noticed before on her journey. Up above, the trill of a bird could be heard—a skylark? Its song lifted her spirits a trifle. Perhaps the atmosphere within the house would also eventually turn out to be less bleak.

As she topped the rise, the rolling moorland stretched out before her as far as her eye could see—heather-covered, barren, strewn with boulders and stones, yet with the renewal of life visible here also. A circle of gray stone huts arrested her eye. Some of the stones were quite large. The huts possessed no roofs, but even now could give some shelter from the elements. Beatrice decided that after the gallop, she would explore this prehistoric site.

The horse, fidgety because she had stopped, urged her to go on. Beatrice's eyes strayed again to the bright emerald-green patches, shining like jewels amid this barren, wild landscape, and beyond to the strange shape of the mighty tor. Both seemed to be beckoning her, inviting her to explore them. The bracing cold wind, much stronger here, felt refreshing to her body and mind.

Beatrice took a deep breath, as calm was slowly restored to her heart. Reluctantly she owned to herself that this desolate place possessed a haunting beauty, and its solitude, uninterrupted by too many sights, offered peace.

She patted the horse's sleek neck. "In a moment. I must take my bearings first." The path here joined the moor road proper, but Beatrice had decided to strike out across the heather.

Abruptly she frowned as the sound of horses' hooves interrupted the solitude. A solitary horseman was riding up the road.

Beatrice waited until the rider was abreast of her. Was he a caller to Brook Manor? The man, attired in a hussar uniform, was tall and rather handsome, with green eyes, sensuous lips, and a patrician nose.

He saluted smartly. "I had no notion the moor would present me with such a beautiful surprise today," he said in a practiced, polished manner. "Could you possibly be—"

"Yes, I am Lady Brook," Beatrice said, smiling.

"It is a great pleasure and honor to make your acquaintance, ma'am," he said. "And may I add, Brook has made an excellent choice. You are a diamond of the first water."

Beatrice felt ridiculously pleased at this compliment. In London she would hardly have spared a thought to such a commonplace, but here, it seemed, one must treasure kind words.

"You have the advantage of me, sir," she said, wondering who he could be. "Ought I to know you? Are you our neighbor perhaps? And were you calling on us?"

"Yes and no. I was going to Brook Manor, but in search of Camilla. I am a houseguest of Sir Oliver, her brother. My name is Tremblay, Captain Eric Tremblay, at your service." He saluted again.

Beatrice's countenance involuntarily darkened upon hearing Camilla's name.

The captain was quick to perceive her change of expression. "Has she set your back up?"

Beatrice smiled ruefully. "Is it so plainly visible?"

"I could discern it, whereas others wouldn't. But then, I know Camilla, and I know her secret, which of course is no secret at all. Only nobody talks about it."

"Secret? What secret?" asked Beatrice with an unpleasant foreboding.

"If you promise not to reveal your knowledge, I shall explain things to you, which would make her conduct a trifle easier to bear and perhaps to understand. Let us ride across the heather." They turned their horses off the road, Beatrice's heart pounding uncomfortably.

"First I must explain," Captain Tremblay said, "that I am a comparative stranger here and, may I add, a stranger to the *ton*. I have been soldiering these many years and hardly ever set foot in London. I met Sir Oliver, a splendid chap, in London at the start of my furlough, and he invited me here. Now, I have a knack for discovering things, and I soon discovered why Camilla was so put out on hearing of Lord Brook's upcoming nuptials. You see, the Swinton family and Lord Brook's are very close."

"Yes. That part I comprehend. Miss Swinton is an old friend of the family."

"She had been much more than that. Almost from

the cradle on, she regarded herself as the future Lady Brook.''

"What!" Beatrice cried in great shock.

"Indeed. That had been the fondest dream of both families. And before Lord Brook went off to war, he and Camilla became affianced.''

"Ohh.'' Beatrice almost lost her hold on her mount in her surprise. "Ohh,'' she repeated in dawning understanding. "No wonder she hates me.''

Captain Tremblay nodded. "Everybody was delighted with the match, everybody expected it. The neighbors, the servants. May I add that Mrs. Teswick's sister is Camilla's old nurse and abigail.''

"Ahh.''

"Of course they would resent you. They cannot help doing so.''

"But why . . . why then did she cry off?''

Tremblay shrugged his shoulders. "Ah, that I do not know. And pray don't breathe a word of it to anybody. Pretend you are not aware of it at all. I do not know the reason behind the termination of the engagement, but it must have been a good one. So your marrying Brook has put her quite out.''

"Yes, but *I* did not know of it. There is no reason why they should hate me. Mrs. Teswick, for instance.''

"Mrs. Teswick, more so than most, is very clannish. And people *do* resent strangers who intrude into their midst. Even such a lovely stranger as yourself.''

"I am exceedingly grateful to you, Captain, for explaining everything," Beatrice said warmly. "It will make things so much easier to bear.''

"Has it been so very bad?'' he asked, with ready sympathy showing in his eyes. "Do not be distressed by their conduct. They will come about. As for Camilla . . .'' He shook his head. "For whatever reason, the termination of this engagement was a sad blow to her. It must pain her a great deal to see *you* in the place she had once hoped would be hers.''

''Yes, yes, that is quite understandable. It's a wonder that she still calls at Brook Manor.''

''Is she there, ma'am?''

''Oh no, she has left already. She was going riding on the moor.'' Beatrice glanced over the vast expanse. ''I have no notion where, or in which direction.''

''Then my errand is all for naught,'' said the captain. ''No, I'll amend that. Meeting such an Incomparable as you was well worth my ride over.''

He carried on in that vein, and Beatrice could not help succumbing to his charm. He had even made her laugh. Then, regretfully, he took his leave of her. ''I must search for Camilla,'' he explained. ''If she has left Brook Manor, I know where she might have gone next. Now, pray remember, don't divulge what I have told you. Good day to you, Lady Brook. Meeting you has been a real pleasure, and I hope I shall see you again soon.'' He saluted, veered around, and cantered off in the opposite direction.

Beatrice stared after him with regret. What a pleasant man, she thought. Well, at least she had three gentlemen who were friendly toward her—Edgar, the squire, and the captain. And it was something to feel cheerful about.

Her spirits fell, however, as she abruptly thought of the intelligence the captain had given her. Her husband and Camilla—affianced. What an unpleasant taste that left in her mouth. Ugh! Why had Camilla cried off? she wondered. And realized Camilla would do all she could to make life miserable for her. That toplofty woman.

Without realizing it, Beatrice spurred the horse to a gallop. And he had not to be urged twice. He took off like a streak, heading straight for the large circular emerald patch of moss and rushes, which hid one of the most treacherous mires in this part of the moor.

And the sky became suddenly overcast.

The trill of the songbird was heard no longer. Only a buzzard soared ominously overhead.

And the horse under Beatrice was galloping straight for the quagmire.

Eight

Beatrice welcomed the cold wind whipping her face as she galloped across the moor. Usually the exhilaration of a gallop brought a shine to her eyes, but today they glittered with a savage desire to find relief for her turbulent emotions in a wild, unrestrained ride.

Only for a moment the thought occurred to her that she was reacting much too strongly to the startling tale she had just heard. The thought vanished instantly. After her encounter with Camilla and Mrs. Teswick, she was in no mood for reasoning or introspection. Hardly aware of her surroundings, she only vaguely registered the fact that a thin drizzle began to fall. Did not register at all that the mist, hanging on the horizon, began now to roll in over the moor.

On she galloped over the damp soggy ground, the horse's hooves sending splashes of mud over its flanks and her riding dress. If she noticed this, she did not care.

Abruptly she was forced to take notice, as the gray's hooves sank deep into the soft marshy ground. The horse reared and plunged with fright. Too late Beatrice perceived the danger.

Her heart leapt in horror and fear. They were in the bog. Visions of riders engulfed with their horses rose before her eyes. Her mouth went dry. Her throat constricted. She must not let that happen to her, it flashed through her mind as she struggled to keep her seat and calm the plunging animal.

But she must dismount. With their combined weight, they would sink that much sooner. The squire's words came to her: once an animal starts struggling, it is done for. And if the horse started sinking, he would pull her under.

Panic gripped her by the throat, threatened to paralyze her. She fought it down. She must stay calm.

The horse kept floundering and plunging, trying to get back to hard ground, so far without much success. Beatrice, utilizing all her skill, contrived to slide off its back in an undignified manner. No sooner had her feet hit the ground then they sank deep into the green sphagnum, causing a fresh wave of panic to wash over her. She swayed, but kept her balance.

She must not struggle. She must keep moving, she recalled the squire's admonition. The slime was now up to her ankles.

She made a few steps, with each step sinking in deeper, still hanging on to the reins. But the horse was struggling, trying to extricate himself. She had to get away from him, for in his thrashing he might knock or pull her down. And then she would be sucked under for sure.

Abruptly the animal's thrashing tore the reins from her hand. The jerk caused her to almost lose her balance. She swayed and flailed her arms—and sank knee-deep into the mire.

She screamed in terror. Panic held her in its grip. The squire's advice rang in her ears: "Keep going at all costs."

Heart pounding, throat dry, eyes dilated in horror, Beatrice sucked up one foot and placed it in front of her. Only to sink in still deeper. She plucked up the other foot and followed through. Her long mud-soaked skirt hampered her progress. Beatrice lifted it and again took a few steps forward.

Forward? She should go *back*, not forward, she realized abruptly. But which way was back? Only now she became aware of the fog closing in on her, shrouding everything in sight. Even the horse, floundering beside her, seemed like a shadowy figure. Yet his hooves were not shadows, and when he struck out . . . She must get away.

Liberally splashed with mud, her skirt heavy and dragging, Beatrice took a step away from the animal, hoping she was heading in the right direction. Alas, she was going even deeper into the mire.

Now she could no longer see the horse, and even his neighing became muffled. Keep going at all costs; the squire's words had seared themselves into her mind.

The muddy, moss-filled ooze was now reaching her thighs.

Keep going. . . .

The pounding of her heart was choking her. The mist made it difficult to breathe. Or was it the panic? She must stay calm.

She forced herself to struggle on—against the grip of panic and the mud. Somehow she must get back to hard ground. Yet she was completely disoriented.

She walked on, with difficulty, but the mud was closing in on her. Against reason, she began to struggle. The urge to flee was overwhelming. But the mire held on tenaciously. Beatrice fought off a wave of hysteria. How could she keep moving? The mud was reaching to her waist! she abruptly realized, and gave another horror-stricken shriek. And flailed her arms wildly.

Abruptly she felt a sharp pain and screamed again. She had struck something. Struck? A solid object.

She whirled around, or tried to. Out of the mist loomed the shape of a rock. A rock—safety. Relief flooded over her. If only she could hang on to it until this fog lifted. She tried to grab the slimy moss-and-lichen-covered surface. Struggling closer, she contrived to scramble onto a precarious perch, hugging the rock, thankful that her feet were out of the mire. Now, if only this fog would lift.

Suddenly she realized that she was shivering with cold. She was chilled through, not only from the mud but also from the rain that now fell steadily, making her situation much graver.

Oh, no, she groaned in despair. The mud will be even worse.

Perhaps it's just a short spring shower, she prayed, as her teeth chattered with cold and fear. She must stay here and wait until the fog lifted. She could not go on, or she might sink even deeper into the morass and . . . and suffocate.

Evelyn had been right to be afraid of this place, she reflected bitterly as she recalled how comforted she had felt at first, riding on the moor. And now, from a friend that had brought her solace, the moor had turned into an enemy seeking to embrace her to death.

She shivered and experienced a fresh wave of panic as she felt her hands and arms slide off the cold, slimy rock. She screamed in terror and hugged the rock tighter. But her limbs were getting numb from cold. The wind was biting sharply through her wet riding dress. How could she hold on thus? How long before her numb body lost its grip on the rock and slipped off into the morass and certain death?

She closed her eyes and prayed for deliverance.

Nine

"Beatrice, Beatrice . . ." The muffled cry came to
Beatrice's ears as if from a great distance. She stirred,
opened her eyes, and listened. Hope leapt up in her
heart. Then a dreadful thought occurred to her. Was she
hallucinating?

She must be. For she fancied it was the voice of her
husband. But it could not be.

"Beatrice!" The voice sounded a trifle closer. It *was*
Gareth.

"I'm here," she cried, the cry ending on a scream as
she almost lost her hold on the rock. "Gareth, Gareth, I
am here," she cried. She pricked up her ears, but heard
nothing. Strained her eyes, but could see nothing save
the swirling wreaths of mist.

"Beatrice!" This time the voice was definitely closer
—and it was Gareth's.

"Gareth, Gareth," she sobbed with relief. "Help!"

A dark shape loomed out of the mist but still seemed
very far away.

"Beatrice, where are you?"

"I'm here, on this rock," she cried. "Help me."
She let go of the rock and began to slide back into the
mud.

His voice came sharp and urgent. "Don't move, stay
where you are. Wait for my directions."

Beatrice hugged the rock again. She stared at the

shadowy figure of her husband. Never had she seen a
more welcome sight.

"Can you see me well?" he shouted.

"Yes," she shouted back.

"I cannot come any closer, or I might have difficulty
extricating us both. I shall throw you a rope. See if you
can catch it."

Something came snaking on the wet air. The rope fell
short of her grasp. He tried again. This time Beatrice,
stretching out her arm, caught it.

"Tie the rope around your waist," the baron commanded.

Beatrice's numb hands had difficulty performing this
task, but at last she had done it.

"Now start walking toward me, and don't be afraid if
you sink. I shall pull you forward."

No longer afraid, and happy in spite of shaking with
cold, Beatrice let herself slide into the mud—to be
engulfed by it almost up to her waist. But this time the
morass held no terror for her, because a lifeline held her
to her husband.

She attempted to walk.

"Don't struggle. Keep calm," admonished her
Gareth. He began to pull her forward. Beatrice, holding
on to the rope, was trying to help him.

Slowly, agonizingly slowly, she was being pulled
toward him. And then, she was standing, still up to her
hips in the mud, but standing, safe within his protecting
arms. Joy now flooded her heart.

He held her close for a brief moment. "You mutton-
headed idiot," he muttered savagely while his lips for an
instant touched her matted hair.

What a relief to have arrived in time, the baron was
thinking. When the squire had caught up with him and
apprised him of the possibility that his wife might venture
out upon the moor on his own horse, he had experienced a
great surge of apprehension. Apprehension? No, not

apprehension, stark naked fear that she might do it, and, unacquainted with the moor, come to grief.

Why? Why was he so concerned? She had served his purpose. But she was a human being. Of course he would be concerned about anybody in like circumstances. To the same extent? With the same intensity of feeling? Could he . . . ?

No, no. Absurd even to think of that.

He owned that he liked her, he admired her spirit and her skill with the ribbons, and he felt responsible for her. After all, he had transplanted her from the comparatively safe environment of London into an unfamiliar place, which spelled danger to the unwary. Of course he would be concerned. It was quite natural. But that was all there was to it.

He released her somewhat roughly.

"Hold on to me. I cannot yet carry you," he said. She realized that he was up to his knees in the tenacious quagmire. "We must try to make haste, for in no time this rain will make it worse."

Holding on to the baron, supported by his strong arm, she struggled to manage a slow walk. Where did he find the strength for it, after his fall yesterday? Beatrice wondered for a moment, before concentrating wholly on her own walking. It was difficult, most difficult, but Gareth seemed to know precisely where he was going.

"How can you see in this mist?" she asked.

"Those few outcroppings give me bearing," he told her. "I am well acquainted with the bogs. I know every inch of the moor. The mire is very deep only in certain places, and I know them. The rain should stop soon and the mist disperse."

It seemed to be taking them forever to get back to hard ground. "Are we . . . are we going in the right direction?" Beatrice asked through chattering teeth as she struggled along in the mud.

"Yes, never fear. I can discern those small outcroppings."

Beatrice blinked. Indeed she could now see a few shadowy outlines. "But . . . but I cannot see Fencer," it abruptly occurred to her.

"He had extricated himself and bolted home. And lucky for you that he did," he added savagely. "You shall never, *never* mount him again. Do you hear? Never."

Beatrice could not see his features clearly, but his tone revealed his anger plainly enough. He must have been livid.

"I allow nobody, but nobody, to ride Fencer."

"Well, I don't see why I cannot ride him, when Miss Swinton can," Beatrice snapped. She was recovering her spirit.

"What?" She felt him stiffen. "Did she tell you that?" he asked incredulously.

"Yes. At least . . . that is what I understood. I—" Abruptly she felt faint. The cold and the different emotions were taking their toll. She swayed. And the next moment he had picked her up and was carrying her as if she were made of feathers. And *that* after his own accident, Beatrice thought with sudden admiration.

"Your injuries, my lord," she cried.

"They are of no consequence."

"But our combined weight—"

"The depth of the mire isn't so great here. We are getting out of the bog."

Beatrice relaxed against his broad shoulder. "Thank God," she whispered. "And thank *you*, Gareth, for saving me." In spite of the cold, she felt strangely contented in his arms.

"My lord, thank God you did it!" Beatrice heard cries of relief and lifted her head.

Several figures materialized out of the mist. Lord

Brook's groom and two others, with horses standing by.

Ready hands stretched out to help them. Lord Brook allowed Hickley to take Beatrice from him, while he mounted a horse. Beatrice noticed with unease that he had some difficulty doing so. Then he commanded Beatrice to be placed in front of him and a blanket to be tucked around her. And the whole troop sloshed across the moor to the road. There a closed carriage was waiting for them, and in a few moments the baron and Beatrice were inside, safe from the elements.

Beatrice, still shuddering with cold, nestled close to her husband for warmth, and he, putting his arm around her shoulders, pressed her close to him and pulled the blanket over her.

"You must never do such a harebrained thing again. Never, do you hear?" he hissed in her ear.

"But . . . but," began Beatrice, "if Camilla can—"

"*Miss* Swinton knows the moor as well as I. You don't. And until you do, you keep to the roads. Riding right into the bog . . . If you don't have enough sense to realize the significance of rushes and green moss, you should not venture—"

"If I were paying attention," Beatrice said, nettled, "I would have perceived I was riding into a marshy ground, but I wasn't paying attention. I was lost in thought."

"People who are lost in thought while riding or walking on the moor may lose their heads," said the baron dryly. "The moor is a place of beauty, but untamed. And it can be dangerous."

Beatrice felt anger stirring within her at his scold. Yet how could she be angry with someone who was warming her shivering body with his own, and more important, who had just saved her from a certain death?

"How did you know where to find me? And how came you to be looking for me?" she asked.

"The squire caught up with me on the moor. He told

me of your wish to ride Fencer, and also that you might be taking a ride on the moors. That was enough to fetch me back posthaste. When I returned and found you gone . . . It was folly, utter folly,'' he said in a harsh voice.

"Well, yes," conceded Beatrice handsomely, "but you needn't rub it in. I should have watched where I was heading. But how did you know I would be there, in that place?"

"You wouldn't have come to any great harm in the smaller mires, and I fancied you had had no time to reach the other dangerous bogs. And when I saw Fencer riderless, I knew that was the most likely place to look for you." He did not mention the fear and despair he had experienced upon seeing the riderless horse.

Beatrice twisted within the circle of his arm to peer into his face. "How shall I ever thank you for saving my life?"

"By never riding Fencer and never venturing upon the moor alone. Not until you are well acquainted with its safe and dangerous places."

"I don't see why you so object to my taking Fencer. I had no trouble riding him. Of course, I *should* have asked your permission. But I'll have my own mount soon, so it's not likely I shall wish to ride him again. As for not going on the moor alone—when I'm told in which direction it is safe for me to do so, I do not see why I shouldn't."

Abruptly she realized he was gazing at her with a singular expression in his dark eyes. Or so she thought. "You are a remarkable woman, Beatrice," he said. "You should be prostrate after such a dreadful ordeal."

"Well, I own I am a trifle shaky," Beatrice said with a slight laugh. "But mostly I am cold."

"It's a hot bath for you, and bed with hot bricks in it," he said with concern. "I just hope you haven't caught a cold. I shall send for Dr. Maynard."

"No. No need to. This is not the first time I have been

exposed to the elements, though I never had a mud bath before," she added with a chuckle.

She closed her eyes suddenly as she relived the horror of her experience afresh. "It was . . . dreadful. I was never so afraid in my life. You may be sure I shall be very careful from now on."

He pulled her closer to him and drew up the blanket, which had slipped. "There is mud on your nose," he said, and taking out his handkerchief, proceeded to wipe it off.

Strange, he did not feel his injuries at all, it suddenly dawned on him. They would hurt like the devil later, of course. But now—he had forgotten them.

"There is mud on your coat. Oh, Gareth," Beatrice cried abruptly, "there is mud all over you." She glanced at herself. "I must look a perfect fright. And the servants shall have a time of it, trying to clean our clothes."

"The servants are paid to do it. And you look delightful."

"It cannot be. You must be funning." Beatrice tried to read his thoughts in his countenance. The blanket had slipped off again. Her rain-soaked garment, sticking to her body, revealed the contours of her shapely breasts.

The baron was very conscious of that fact. Very conscious of his wife's lovely face upturned to his, her large blue eyes regarding him with uncertainty, her inviting lips inches away from his own.

And he forgot his resolution. Involuntarily he bent his head and his lips sought hers, hesitating at first, then more ruthlessly, hungrily.

And Beatrice? She had been kissed before. But never like this. Roderick's kisses, enjoyable though they were, paled into insigificance beside her husband's passion. Or did the proximity of death add special savor to the experience?

She had no thought of a closer relationship with her

husband-in-name-only. She, who had vowed to give herself only to the man she loved, had never dreamed that she would welcome Gareth's kisses. But after the initial shock of feeling his hot lips upon hers, she forgot herself. Forgot how tired and cold she was. Her arms went about his neck and her lips responded willingly to his kiss.

But only for an instant. The next, a loud shout and the face of a rider appearing in the carriage window tore them apart. Edgar, concerned and anxious, was peering into the carriage from the back of his horse. "Uncle, Beatrice," he cried.

The baron lowered the window. "Beatrice is well," he said curtly. "As for me—you must be disappointed again."

"Uncle," cried Edgar, seemingly hurt to the raw.

Lord Brook put up the window, and Edgar was left to ride beside the carriage without any further conversation.

"He must have discovered what occurred and ridden after us," said Beatrice.

"Yes. It is still broad daylight," said the baron with a sneer.

Beatrice's warm feelings and admiration for her husband burst like a pricked balloon. She even felt vexed at her response to his kiss. "Why do you keep alluding to his fear?" she said with reproach. "He cannot help himself."

The baron's mouth tightened to a grim line. "He is a coward and a cur," he said with contempt and loathing.

"My lord, how can you? He is your nephew," cried Beatrice, quite appalled.

"A regrettable fact. Otherwise he would not be residing at Brook Manor."

"Why do you hate him so, Gareth? Why? What has he done to you?"

Lord Brook's countenance hardened. His voice had a

cold, metallic ring. "Enough. Some things are none of your concern. And this is one of them."

"But—" began Beatrice, dismayed.

"Enough, I said," he repeated harshly. "I shan't tolerate meddling, and your passing judgment—"

"I was not passing judgment," retorted Beatrice hotly. "I was—"

Abruptly everything turned dismal and gray for her, like the mist-shrouded moors. She felt tired, cold, and discouraged. For a moment she had fancied a warm and loving human being cared for her. But that was just an illusion. Why would he kiss her thus? The chaste peck he had given her during the wedding ceremony was so different from the hot, passionate pressure of his lips today. Was he also caught up in the reaction caused by her close brush with death?

Hot tears pricked at her eyelids. "I'm sorry, my lord," she said in a strangled voice. "I wasn't judging, or prying, or . . . or anything. It is my besetting sin— speaking what comes to my mind. I shall try to watch my tongue in the future."

She shouldn't be so humble with him, she should fight and snap back; but suddenly she was just too tired. She shut her eyes, and pulling away from him, leaned back against the squabs. Thus, in uncomfortable silence, each in his own corner of the chaise, they arrived at Brook Manor.

Ten

After having a hot bath and being tucked into a warm
bed by her maid, Beatrice felt a little less gloomy. Her
own bruises and injuries she discounted as naught. But
she was worried about the baron. Only when Dr. Maynard arrived to examine her, and assured her that Lord
Brook, though sore, had not done any real damage to
his old wounds, did she relax.

"He shouldn't set out so soon on a journey, but of
course, he will," said the doctor. "Well, we must trust
that his iron constitution will withstand that too. But
one day he *shall* go too far."

Edgar, whom she saw later that day, was of the same
opinion. "Uncle refuses to admit that he cannot go on
as before. And one day it will kill him," was his way of
putting it. Greatly concerned, and apologetic for distressing Beatrice, he nevertheless felt he ought to warn
her to prepare for the inevitable.

He explained to her that Lord Brook had once excelled in sports, but had injured his arm and leg yet
refused to accept the limitations his injuries placed upon
him—with the inevitable disastrous results.

Beatrice also discovered from Edgar that her husband
had sustained those injuries in a vulgar fight or a duel—
both equally deplorable, in her opinion. Of course,
Edgar did not tell her that in so many words. He implied
it inadvertently in the conversation, before he caught
himself.

The baron kept to his chamber the rest of that day—the doctor had ordered him to rest if he intended to start out tomorrow—and Beatrice, feeling a trifle shaky still, retired early to bed. But again she could not fall asleep, her thoughts dwelling on her husband. He could not be in love with her, yet he found her attractive when she was disheveled and covered with mud. She did not love him, of course, she hardly knew him. The emotion of the moment had carried her away, carried them both away. But he had risked injury and his life to save her. That should put her forever in his debt. It was too bad his rudeness had to spoil the good impression he had made on her.

Beatrice's conviction that her husband's passionate kiss in the carriage was simply the result of overwrought nerves was confirmed when on the following day—a Sunday—Lord Brook treated her in a reserved and cold manner. He behaved, in fact, as if that scene in the carriage had never taken place.

After breakfast they all went to church, though the baron was reluctant to attend the service. Beatrice soon discovered why, when they entered the village—although he seemed to treat the whole matter with cold indifference.

The village of Melton Combe was a delightful little place with its whitewashed rose-covered thatched cottages clustered around a village green. The cottage gardens were a riot of spring color, the scent of flowers filling the air.

Dominating the village green was a fifteenth-century granite church. Framed by many trees in their spring finery, and with the sun shining brightly out of the blue sky, the cottages and church presented a charming sight.

The parishioners, however, were anything but charming. Most of them—ladies and gentlemen and plain poor moor people alike—though evincing curiosity, seemed to go out of their way to avoid her husband and herself. Those few who could not avoid meeting them received the baron's greetings and his introductions to Beatrice with cold politeness, imperfectly concealing their hostility.

Why? What had she ever done to them? And why was her husband so disliked by his neighbors? Only the squire remained his genial, friendly self, and he, the captain, and Camilla's dandy brother, Sir Oliver, were full of admiration for Beatrice and showed their concern upon hearing of her adventure.

When Beatrice, with others, was walking back to the carriage after the service was over, the squire contrived to pull her aside, and lowering his voice, said, "Wished to tell you this before. Brook had sustained some bad injuries to his arm and leg, which account for his black moods sometimes. You must try to understand. He did not tell you of that? Or how he received them?"

"He did not elaborate. But I do know how he came by them."

"You must not ask him about it, or mention it. He does not wish to speak of it."

"As if I would," said Beatrice, wondering how the squire could suppose she would cross-question her husband about some sordid fight or even a so-called affair of honor.

Shortly after, she was riding back home, with only herself and Albinia in the carriage. Her husband had ridden to church, and Sir Oliver had invited Edgar over to Swinton Court.

Beatrice could not contain her puzzlement any longer. Utilizing the opportunity of being alone with Albinia, she said, "I cannot comprehend why most people are so hostile to Gareth. Pray tell me, or I shall be obliged to ask him. And I would rather not."

"I should say not. He would not tell you. He cannot be proud of what he did." Her lips compressed in a tight, disapproving line. Then she gave an exasperated sigh. "You might as well find out about it now—you'll be bound to discover it sooner or later. The people are incensed at Brook, and rightly so, because he was affianced to Camilla. It was an arrangement of long standing, was made when they both were in short-coats and—"

"Well, yes, I do know that they were engaged and she cried off."

"No, she didn't. He did."

"What!" exclaimed Beatrice, much astounded, her eyes round with shock.

"You may well stare. I have never been so mortified in my life. My own brother doing the unthinkable for a gentleman, crying off from an engagement."

"But . . . but a gentleman simply doesn't do that. No matter how much he might regret his decision to offer for the lady."

"Well, *he* did. You cannot wonder now we never receive any callers and people avoid us like the plague."

"Why would he do it, then? For what reason?"

Albinia shrugged her shoulders pettishly. "All my maid was able to discover was that they had words the night before. Brook was in a shocking temper, not an unusual thing for him since Waterloo. But not a word of explanation would he accord to *me*. No reason for his shocking conduct. Poor Edgar was quite overwhelmed, not to mention *my* wounded feelings . . ."

Beatrice hardly listened to the rest of Albinia's complaints. Lord Brook had cried off. Why? How *could* he? And the *ton* knew. That's why they cut him. He had put himself beyond the pale with his action. Why? What had compelled him to do so? Oh, Beatrice did not wonder that he did not wish to wed Camilla after all. That was hardly surprising to her. But not liking one's chosen bride had nothing to do with a gentleman's code of honor. Gareth's act, so contrary to that code, must lower him in her eyes. She recalled his dislike of the female sex. But that alone wouldn't answer. Or did he find Camilla too masterful?

Beatrice felt keen disappointment in her husband. And yet . . . She recalled the warmth of his lips upon her own. Recalled being carried by him, in spite of what she knew must have been quite a painful ordeal for him. Like and dislike warred in her breast. If only she knew why he had broken his engagement. But of course she could never ask him. Neither could she ask Camilla.

In a very vexed and dissatisfied mood, Beatrice returned to Brook Manor.

Eleven

Beatrice gazed out the window of her chamber at the
bleak slope of the moor. The weather had changed
again. The sky was overcast and the cold wind blowing
in through the open window penetrated her light blue
silk gown. Hardly aware of what she was doing, she
shut the window and kept staring out, thinking of
Gareth. She wished he would not set out today on his
journey. He had seemed a little stiff as he swung himself
out of the saddle upon their return from church. What
was this urgent matter that forced him to leave his home
when not in the best of health?

She heaved a sigh. When she had made her decision to
marry him, she thought she would not become involved
in his affairs, would not care what he did with his time,
as long as he left her alone. Now, only a few days after
the wedding, she found herself wishing to know the
reason behind all of his actions.

So sunk in thought was she that at first she did not
hear the timid knock on the door of her bedchamber.
When the knock was repeated, however, a trifle louder,
she turned away from the window with an expression of
annoyance. "Pray come in," she called out. For an
instant her heart leapt up at the thought it might be her
husband. Then she shook her head. He would never
knock on the door with such timidity.

The door opened to reveal the apprehensive face of

Jean, the kitchen maid whom she had rescued from the housekeeper.

The child hesitated on the threshold, casting her large frightened eyes at Beatrice.

Beatrice frowned. "Is the work in the sewing room not to your liking, or has Mrs. Teswick been bullying you again?" she asked.

"Oh, no, no, ma'am. I be that glad to work in the sewing room."

"Well then, what? Pray come in and shut the door."

The girl obeyed, giving her a deep curtsy. "I . . . I beg your ladyship's pardon for disturbing your ladyship, but . . . but . . . Oh pray, milady, help poor Alice. She can't help being sick, and Mrs. Teswick will make her work until she drops dead. She's got two little ones who would be left motherless, but that don't concern Mrs. Teswick."

Beatrice's frown deepened. "Well, shut the door and tell me precisely who Alice is and what Mrs. Teswick is forcing her to do."

She seated herself in an armchair by the window and beckoned the child to a footstool beside her.

Jean perched on the stool uneasily, awed by the grandeur of the chamber and overwhelmed by her own boldness. Her story was not quite coherent, but at the end of twenty minutes Beatrice had gotten enough out of her to be very angry indeed.

Alice worked as one of the upstairs maids, and because she was a weak, thin young woman, some chores were beyond her strength. From Jean's description it sounded as if the poor woman was in the first stages of consumption. She had no strength to lift the heavy burdens or shift the massive furniture about. She had done so, however, before the babies came; then she grew progressively weaker.

Mrs. Teswick, herself never ill in her life, scolded Alice severely and called her a malingering good-for-nothing.

Beatrice decided to speak to the housekeeper at once.

A few moments later Mrs. Teswick, her eyes glittering with hatred, her attitude one of defiance, stood before Beatrice, arms crossed on her chest. "You wished to see me, madam," she said, imperfectly concealing the hostility in her voice.

"Yes, Mrs. Teswick. It has come to my attention that Alice, the upstairs maid, is not well and cannot carry out her duties."

"Has she come sniveling to you?" asked the housekeeper, wrath gathering in her eyes.

"She has not come to me for help. It's of no consequence how I know about her, but I do. She should be given lighter work."

"If she cannot perform her duties, she will be turned off," said the housekeeper.

Anger surged through Beatrice. "No she won't. I shall talk to Dr. Maynard and ask him what work—if any—she should be permitted to do. In the meantime, she shall retire to her chamber and rest."

"And who should take her place, if I may be permitted to ask?" the housekeeper asked venomously.

"Surely one task can be shared among fifty servants. Pray see to it that Alice is relieved of her present duties until something more fitting is found for her to do."

"If Lord Brook or Miss Risborough wishes it," said the housekeeper, two bright spots burning on her cheeks.

Beatrice's temper threatened to slip its leash completely. She took a deep breath. "Mrs. Teswick, let me make one thing plain to you—again: I shan't allow you to abuse or dismiss the servants. No, I am not about to take over all your duties upon myself or constantly look over your shoulder, but if you persist in your callous disregard of the feelings and health of those under your charge, I shall be forced to take drastic measures."

"You mean you would turn me off?" spat the housekeeper. "You cannot do that. His lordship would not allow it. He is very satisfied with the way I run things."

"He may be, but I'll wager that he never saw the dust on the mantelshelf." Beatrice had noticed dust on the furniture on a few occasions, the last time on the mantelshelf in the hall, and in her own dressing room.

"Dust? What dust? Where?" For the first time Mrs. Teswick's composure seemed to have been shaken. "Where? Just tell me where, and I'll find the person responsible and I'll make sure—"

Beatrice put up a hand. "I don't wish you to punish a specific person. Give them all a warning. That should suffice." Her eyes narrowed in a speculative stare. Could it be . . . ?

She glanced through the open door to the dressing room. There was a faint smudge of dust on the dressing table. She looked at her hands and then around the chamber. "I seem to have misplaced one of my rings," she said. "Pray see if it is on the dressing table."

The housekeeper, puzzled and suspicous, went to search for the ring.

Beatrice was watching her closely. If her eyesight was good, she must notice the dust. But no change of expression registered on the lined countenance. And it took her an inordinately long time to find the ring.

Beatrice released a long breath of understanding. The housekeeper's sight was failing. Had that fact something to do with her harsh treatment of the servants?

"Thank you," she said as she slipped the ring on her finger. "Now, about Alice—"

"I shan't do anything until I have word from his lordship or Miss Risborough," said the housekeeper.

"Very well. Fortunately, Lord Brook hasn't left yet. I shall speak to him immediately. But you could save yourself and me a great deal of bother if you agreed to carry out my orders without opposition."

"I have done my duty to his lordship's satisfaction for many years," said Mrs. Teswick. "He has never had cause to complain. The domestics must be kept in line.''

Beatrice sighed. ''Mrs. Teswick, why are you so averse to showing compassion? Don't you think there might come a time when you might need some?''

A startled look leapt into the old woman's gray eyes. ''Never!'' she cried. And the word came out like an explosion.

She is afraid she will be found out, found inadequate and turned off, Beatrice suddenly realized.

''You may go now, Mrs. Teswick. I shall speak to his lordship, but I wish I were not obliged to do so. Alice must be given a chance to recover.''

She dismissed the housekeeper. What turbulent waters did the downstairs household conceal? she mused as she made her way to the study, where she knew Lord Brook was closeted with a caller.

The caller turned out to be the captain. Beatrice recognized his voice, even though it was raised in anger. Her husband's voice was raised too, but as yet she could not distinguish the words spoken by the men.

She placed her hand on the knob, then hesitated. Should she intrude now? But she might not have another chance before the baron went away. She knocked lightly. The knock was unheeded. Beatrice knocked again, then cautiously opened the door.

The two men were standing in the middle of the room on the red Axminster carpet. It flitted through Beatrice's mind that their stances were very much like those of two fighting cocks, and her lips curved with amusement.

The amusement was chilled at once by the words that she could now hear: ''If you don't do it, I shall kill you for the contemptible thief that you are. I have waited and waited. But I shall wait no longer. My sister will no longer live in shadows, dependent on your largess. She shall have what is rightfully hers. She and the child.''

''If you would but listen, intead of berating me,'' snapped Lord Brook. ''I was unable—''

She must have made a movement—from shock perhaps—for abruptly he turned. "Beatrice," he cried,
"what are you doing here?"

"Wishing for a word with you, my lord. But I can
wait. If you but step into my chamber before you
depart."

"Is it important?" he asked irritably.

"It is important."

He frowned. "Very well. I shall see you later, then."

"Pray forgive me for intruding," Beatrice said, and
shut the door. She was quite shaken by the savage words
and the murderous look of the normally friendly
captain.

What could Gareth have done to his sister that had
sent this pleasant man into such a rage?

In impatience she waited for her husband. When at
last he came, his countenance a vexed question mark,
Beatrice was more concerned with asking him about the
captain than talking to him about Mrs. Teswick and
Alice. But he did not give her time to voice her concern.
"What is it you wish to ask me about? Pray be quick
about it. I must make haste." He was attired for the
journey in an elegant tight-fitting blue coat and
breeches, and was obviously impatient to leave.

"But . . ." Oh, she might as well tell him, although
compared with the captain's threat on his life, Mrs. Teswick's insubordination seemed a trifling matter.

"I wish to talk to you about Mrs. Teswick," she said.

A frown creased his brow. "What has occurred
now?" he said in an irritable voice.

Beatrice's grievance against the servants came to the
fore. "Oh, Gareth," she cried, "you must tell her, tell
all of them, to obey my orders. You must back me up.
Teswick won't listen to anything I say. First it was a
kitchen maid whom she abused dreadfully and wished
to dismiss. Now I discover she is making another
servant, an ill servant, work too hard. And when I

demanded she give the maid another task, she said she takes her orders only from you or your sister. Pray tell her to attend to me.''

Lord Brook's brow knit and his mouth tightened. ''That is not like her. She is always most correct in her conduct. I know she dislikes you because . . . Even so, she *would* mind proprieties. You must have set her back up.''

''But I didn't. Gareth, Alice is a consumptive. She cannot do heavy work.''

''Are you sure of your facts?''

Beatrice nodded. ''Of course.''

''I shall speak to Mrs. Teswick. But you should be able to handle her. You cannot run to me with every domestic trifle.''

''I tell you, she won't listen to me. She hates me.''

''Perhaps you rub her the wrong way. Teswick always seemed a perfect housekeeper to us all.''

''I did not rub her the wrong way. At least, I am not conscious of it. Oh, but I'm sure that when you speak to her she shall mind me. I am very much obliged to you. You don't know how uncomfortable and distressing it is, not to be paid attention to. Oh, I *am* so relieved.''

With that matter disposed of, Beatrice's thoughts turned to the more important overheard quarrel. ''Oh, Gareth, I am so worried. What has occurred?'' she asked. ''Why does Captain Tremblay wish you harm?''

He grimaced. ''He doesn't wish me harm. He—''

''But I disctinctly heard him say that he would kill you. Oh, pray tell me that he won't.''

''Of course he won't. He was three parts disguised. And you shouldn't listen at the keyhole,'' he added unpleasantly. ''What else did you hear?''

''Nothing. Something about his sister. And I didn't eavesdrop,'' she cried indignantly. ''I knocked twice.'' But her concern overcame her indignation. ''Oh, Gareth, pray take care. There was murder in his eyes.''

"Now, don't you make a Cheltenham tragedy out of it," he said scowling. "Forget all about it. This has nothing to do with you."

"But what *is* this all about? I wish to know. What—"

Suddenly she recalled and bit her lip, as unbidden tears sprang to her eyes. "No, never mind. Your affairs are not my concern. After all, our marriage is a business arrangement." Her voice came out strangled from her contracted throat.

And abruptly he was close beside her, gazing deep into her eyes.

"It needn't be," he said in a husky voice.

"I . . . I beg your pardon."

He placed his hand on her shoulder. "Our marriage—it need not be only a business arrangement."

Beatrice shrank back involuntarily, and his hands fell.

"Am I *that* repulsive to you? I thought that in the carriage . . ."

The naked hurt in his eyes, before they were veiled by a cold mask of indifference, touched her deeply. "Repulsive? Why should I find you repulsive? Of course I don't find you repulsive," she cried hotly. "On the contrary . . ."

She hadn't meant to say that. She had surprised herself. She did not love him. She couldn't. And yet . . .

"What . . . What did you say?" he asked hoarsely, grabbing her shoulders and thrusting his face close to hers. His quickened breath felt hot on her face. The grip on her shoulders tightened painfully. His eyes burned with desire. And Beatrice felt suddenly frightened.

She licked her now dry lips. "I . . . I merely said that I found you not unattractive."

"And what do you find attractive in me?" he asked harshly, pushing her away from him. His face mirrored his bitterness. "My limp that comes over me at the most inopportune moments, or my weak arm—the arm once so strong, that cannot regain its strength. Or my face—surely not!"

Beatrice was aghast. Her heart was pounding from some strange emotion. "I don't regard your arm or leg as anything. They are merely a leg and an arm. And I'm sure your old injuries would heal faster and give you less trouble if you would but forget about them in a *reasonable* way. Forget about them, save when you are obliged to drive or ride. Then be sure to remember and act prudently. It's as simple as that. As for not being strong —my lord, you dragged me out of the bog and you carried me. If your limbs could perform *that* feat, then they serve you well indeed."

He seemed much struck by this observation. "True, true. I myself was surprised at the ease with which I carried you. But my face," he abruptly cried.

"Now, that," said Beatrice, her eyes twinkling, "I have a very definite opinion about. I like it."

He blinked. Suddenly his lips pressed shut in a bitter line. "Do not deceive me, Beatrice. I am not considered a handsome man and I know it. Edgar and that damn captain—now, *they* are considered handsome."

"Oh, yes, in the conventional sense they are handsome. But your countenance is striking and exudes strength."

"Beatrice!" It was a cry of incredulity, relief, and dawning joy. And just as swiftly the joyful look vanished, to be replaced by a thundercloud. "You are trying to turn me up sweet for some reason," he said savagely. "But it won't work."

"I am *not* trying to turn you up sweet. Did I not tell you that my besetting sin is speaking my mind. I like you, though I might not like everything you do or say. But whatever I don't like about you, it is certainly not your appearance. I might find repulsive your conduct and your driving in that neck-or-nothing faction, and things of that nature, but not you."

"Beatrice . . ." Abruptly he grabbed her shoulders again and pulled her close, his arms about her as he bent his head and his mouth covered hers in a ruthless, passionate kiss.

Blood pounded in Beatrice's temples, her body tingled with delight. Never had Roderick's kisses given her such a thrill. A river of fire was spreading from his lips and his body through her whole being. And then she ceased even to marvel at that. Released from inhibitions by her marriage vows, she did not seek to curb his hands as they tore at her dress and pushed it off her shoulders.

"Uncle Gareth!" The cry was sharp with consternation. And cold. Like cold water dashed on the heat of their desire.

Instantly Lord Brook released her. His arms fell to his sides. His face became a mask of stone. Only his eyes burned with hatred of his nephew.

And Beatrice? She did not know whether to be furiously angry with Edgar, or grateful and relieved.

"You wished to see me?" Lord Brook asked. His voice was icy cold.

"Yes, Hickley was looking for you. If you mean to start out you'd better make haste. It's raining heavily. And the moor roads might become impassable."

"Much obliged. But," he added with a sardonic curl of his lips, "you were not obliged to seek me out. You could have sent a footman."

Edgar flushed.

"Perhaps I shall wait until the rain ceases. Unlike you, I don't mind venturing out after dark," the baron said with a sneer.

Cold dismay struck Beatrice's heart. There it was again. Mocking the poor man about his fear of the dark. And she had just forgotten her vexation with her husband.

The baron bowed. "Good day, Beatrice. I shall endeavor to be back as soon as I can. We shall continue this discussion when I return." And the look he cast at her spoke volumes.

Beatrice, conscious of her disheveled attire, could only murmur, "Yes, to be sure, my lord. Pray take care."

She observed that he went to the door with a much lighter, springier step than when he came in, and she was glad of it. But not glad of the malevolent look he cast at Edgar on his way out.

"Pray forgive this intrusion, Beatrice," Edgar said in a somewhat shamefaced manner. "I was but thinking of Uncle's welfare," he muttered, and bowed himself out of the chamber.

And Beatrice was left alone with her mixed thoughts and stirred emotions.

Twelve

Later that day Beatrice discovered that her husband had apparently forgotten to speak to the housekeeper about Alice. And Albinia, when appealed to, was not inclined to speak to Mrs. Teswick on the chambermaid's behalf —out of fear, Beatrice suspectd, that her comfortable arrangement with the housekeeper might be overset. As long as all *her* whims were catered to, Teswick could do as she pleased. And Mrs. Teswick still refused to obey Beatrice.

How *could* the housekeeper conduct herself with such gross impropriety as to refuse to carry out and countermand the orders of her mistress? wondered Beatrice. She began to suspect that the housekeeper, if not precisely a prime candidate for Bedlam, was not far removed from it. And with her hatred for Beatrice, it behooved Beatrice to be careful. No telling what a deranged mind could be capable of.

She did not think, however, that her husband would share her opinion of Mrs. Teswick. To him, as to Albinia, Mrs. Teswick was a paragon of a housekeeper, and no matter how he might feel about Beatrice, he would not share her doubts.

Blood rushed to Beatrice's face as she once more recalled Gareth's hot kiss on her lips and his wandering hands. What was the matter with her, she berated herself, to succumb so easily to the strong attraction he held for her?

She had married him with one purpose only. The thought of being obliged to fulfill a wife's childbearing role with a man whom she did not love had filled her with dread, yet when Gareth was about to undress her, it was not fear that had gripped her, but excitement. Even her slight uneasiness and fear of the unknown were lost in the singular feelings he had stirred within her. She was caught up in a strong emotion she had not experienced before, save in a milder way, when he had kissed her in the carriage.

It was all very puzzling. She was not in love with him. He could not be in love with her, yet there in her bed-chamber he had desired her. But she did not wish to be desired without love. Heaving an impatient sigh, she resolved to refrain from asking him to step into her chamber. She would speak to him on neutral ground.

"You are very pensive, Beatrice."

Beatrice came out of her reverie. "I beg your pardon. I was worried about Alice, the chambermaid," she said quickly.

She and Edgar were the only two diners again, with her husband absent and Albinia keeping to her room.

"Oh. And why are you worried about her?" His handsome countenance was friendly and his eyes seemed to follow her every move. He looked very elegant in an olive-green coat and beige pantaloons.

Beatrice pushed her dinner plate away. "Alice is ill and should be given lighter work. But Mrs. Teswick won't hear of it. Gareth has forgotten to speak to her, and Albinia won't."

"Then pray tell me what it is you wish done. Perhaps I can prevail upon Teswick to carry out your wishes."

"You?" It had not occurred to her to ask him.

Edgar's eyes crinkled. "After all, I am not without influence, at least in regard to the domestics. I may not be able to change Uncle Gareth's or Aunt Albinia's habits, but the servants mind me on the odd occasion when I am obliged to give some order or another."

Beatrice's countenance cleared. "Oh, could you speak to Teswick tonight?" she cried.

"Better still, I shall speak to her at once. But not with you present," he added apologetically. "That would set her back up at the onset. Pray wait for me in the drawing room, and I shall ring for her at once. Oh, and pray tell me exactly what it is you wish done."

Beatrice told him, and retired to the drawing room to await with impatience Edgar's interview with Mrs. Teswick.

The result was all she could have hoped for. Edgar came into the drawing room beaming. "It is all settled," he said in a cheerful voice. "Alice shall be given lighter work and Dr. Maynard shall be seeing her regularly until she improves."

"Oh, Edgar, how shall I ever thank you?" she cried, stretching her hand to him impulsively.

Edgar turned somber. "There is a way you could thank me, but I shan't ask you to." And his insistent, steady gaze drove hot blood to Beatrice's cheeks. Just so had Gareth been gazing at her today. But Edgar? Edgar . . . ?

He gave a deprecating short laugh. "Pray forgive me, Beatrice, but you are a very beautiful woman, and I am a man. No, don't be alarmed. I admire you too much to be betrayed into an impropriety. Pray forget what I have just said." For some reason Gareth's phrase, "trying to turn me up sweet," sprang to Beatrice's mind. Still, she had known male admiration, so it wasn't altogether surprising that Edgar found her attractive. It was even pleasant.

He seated himself on the sofa beside her. "If there is anything else you wish done," he said, possessing himself of her hand and pressing it warmly, "pray don't hesitaste to ask me. I shall endeavor my poor best to help you."

He released her hand almost immediately and moved a little away from her. Beatrice relaxed, filled with gratitude. Of course she could trust him to behave with propriety, and she was exceedingly glad that he had been able to arrange matters for Alice.

"I shall not hesitate to do so," she said, her eyes lighting up with warmth. "You are a kind, good man, Edgar, and I am very glad that you have become my nephew-in-law."

"I wouldn't put it quite that way myself," said Edgar with a comical grimace, "but I am gratified that I am permitted to be your friend. I am, am I not?" he added anxiously.

"Of course you are, Edgar. And I shall be very happy to apply to you for help."

And apply she did the very next day, when she had a minor skirmish with the housekeeper again. Edgar contrived once more to arrange matters to her satisfaction. Beatrice, grateful, felt that very soon she would apply to him for help in all matters. He was never boorish or ungracious and was always only too ready and too pleased to oblige.

Not only that, he went out of his way to provide diversion for her, taking her out riding (Beatrice's mount and groom had arrived at last), walking, or else playing backgammon with her when it was raining. He even arranged for a picnic to be held on the moor—a little *al fresco* party; but since those invited included Camilla, Beatrice at first wasn't sure if she welcomed that plan.

The picnic, however, turned out an agreeable affair, especially since Sir Oliver and the captain, not to mention Edgar, went out of their way to please Beatrice, thus greatly displeasing Camilla. So of course Beatrice came to the conclusion that the picnic was a splendid notion after all.

At first she regarded Captain Tremblay with suspicion, mindful of the threats he had made; but his conduct was so amiable, she finally convinced herself he indeed must have been only foxed and therefore belligerent when he had uttered those threats.

They explored the moor and held their picnic at Crockern Tor—once the meeting place of the Stannary Parliament—where numerous slablike rocks provided handy natural tables and chairs. At the end of the meal the conversation turned to Wistman's Wood, an ancient grove of oaks with five-hundred-year-old trees, over which the captain and Edgar, but especially Camilla, waxed quite enthusiastic.

Only Sir Oliver evinced no interest in the ancient copse, saying he was not partial to old trees. Camilla berated him that but for his dawdling over his attire, they would have had the time to go to Wistman's Wood yet today.

Beatrice's interest in the grove was aroused, and she decided to see it at the earliest opportunity. A hike of forty minutes could be undertaken anytime. And no fear of getting lost if she went alone. If she continued in a northerly direction and parallel to the river, she couldn't miss the woods. And if she kept to that route, she wouldn't fall into any bogs either. So nothing untoward could happen to her.

Upon returning to Brook Manor, the picnickers had some tea, and Beatrice, still full of enthusiasm, expressed her wish to go alone to Wistman's Wood. Edgar begged her not to, but to wait and go with him. So did the captain. Only Camilla said scornfully, "A child could find its way there and back with no trouble. I have been there alone scores of times. But then, *I* was born and bred on the moors."

Implying that she herself wasn't, so therefore couldn't, Beatrice thought, gritting her teeth.

Sir Oliver said, "Don't think you could come to any harm. Doubt if you'd get lost. But if you do, if you ever get lost on the moor, don't try finding your way back. Best wait to be rescued—provided people know you went on the moor and which way you went. Still, why not take a footman along, or a groom?''

Camilla said patronizingly, "Perhaps you should indeed wait until somebody can go with you, or take along a servant. Otherwise we might be obliged to set up a search party for you."

Whereupon Beatrice decided at once to go tomorrow to Wistman's Wood—alone. A decision she was later to regret.

Thirteen

Beatrice, a picnic basket slung over her arm, was striding across the heather, enjoying the sunshine and the fresh air. As yesterday, the moor seemed a friendly place, wild and lonely to be sure, but peaceful and non-theatening under the blue sky.

It was late afternoon, but she was sure she would be home well before sunset. She had intended to start out right after breakfast, but first a minor skirmish with Mrs. Teswick delayed her, and then Camilla and Oliver arrived, bearing Edgar off with them. Edgar had begged her to wait until he could accompany her, but she had decided against it. She also declined to have a servant accompany her. It had become a matter of pride with her to go to Wistman's Wood alone.

After the callers and Edgar had gone, Beatrice picked up the picnic basket, which she had asked Pedmore to order Gaston to prepare, and set out across the moor. She could get used to living here, she thought as she strolled along the path she had trod yesterday. One just had to watch out for the bogs. And Beatrice would certainly give those shiny emerald patches a wide berth.

As for witches, pixies, and such like that Jean, on fetching Beatrice her mended dress, had warned her about—Beatrice paid no attention to such silly talk. Any old wood was bound to be "inhabited" by legendary creatures.

As she walked along, Beatrice considered how her life had changed. Just recently she would never have thought it possible, but her mental picture of Roderick was fading fast. A slight sadness for what might have been still lingered perhaps; but he belonged now to the past that she was done with. And on a bright day like today, the future must look promising.

So she strode on, in reasonably good spirits, her only worry being about her husband's safe return home. She wished she knew where Gareth had gone *this* time. And owned to a slight feeling of pique because she did not know it.

On she strode among heather, gorse, and whortleberry bushes, among moss-covered boulders and rocks, with the wind whistling about her head and the sound of the West Dart, rushing and tumbling along its course, striking her ears pleasantly. Crossing the river by the stepping-stones, she continued north toward Longaford Tor, scanning the steep boulder-strewn slopes of the river valley. Already in the distance—though she was still far away—she could see a splash of green, the copse of trees hugging the slope.

Like yesterday, Beatrice found the hiking a trifle hard on her feet and legs. Today they ached even more than yesterday. She decided to rest and have her picnic before proceeding further.

Spreading a small tablecloth on the ground on a large flat boulder, she sat down and enjoyed her meal. Cold chicken and bread and butter, and preserves, with a bottle of wine. The preserves tasted a trifle bitter— perhaps not enough sugar had been added—but she ate the meal with relish, the fresh air and her walk having whetted her appetite.

After the repast she found herself suddenly sleepy. She glanced about the lonely moor. No one in sight. Well, a pony somewhere in the distance, and she fancied she saw some sheep and a cow, but no human presence.

It would scarcely matter if she had a nap, even though on a not very comfortable bed. But not a cold one, the stone having been warmed by the sun.

She curled up on her stone bench, resting her shoulders and head against the picnic basket, and hardly had she snuggled into a more comfortable position than she was fast asleep. The sun kept shining and the stream rushing, the buzzards soaring overhead. Beatrice slept.

The sun was dipping down, the sky became overcast, and the mist was rising from the river. Still Beatrice slept on.

A fine drizzle began to fall and night descended on the moor.

The cold wind picked up and the rain now fell heavily as the swollen stream tumbled angrily over the stones.

Beatrice remained asleep.

Beatrice awoke shivering in pitch darkness, rain was beating down mercilessly on her unprotected body. She stirred groggily and for a moment could not comprehend where she was. Then the wet, cold stone recalled her. She had fallen asleep, but . . . How could it be? It was nighttime already.

She touched her head and sat up stiffly. Had she slept that long? Impossible. She must get back. Her teeth chattered with cold. But how to go back? It was pitch dark, and the river must be swollen. She couldn't jump across the stepping-stones now. No doubt there was a roundabout way of returning home, but she might get lost.

Sir Oliver's words rang in her mind: "When lost, stay where you are and wait to be rescued." But she had to get out of the rain. Her bewilderment and grogginess were replaced by rising panic. She was alone on the moor again, and it had turned hostile once more. But this time it was her fault. Or was it? She couldn't have slept that long. Unless . . . Had she been drugged?

Laudanum in the preserves? She must not become fanci-
ful, she scolded herself. And she must get out of the
rain. She picked up her picnic basket and rose to her
feet. She must make for the wood to find shelter from
the driving rain. Mist now shrouded the river so heavily
she could hardly see it, but the dark mass of Wistman's
Wood was clearly discernible.

Beatrice started forward and up, but the picnic basket
hampered her progress. The steep, soggy incline was not
easy to negotiate in the dark. She needed both hands
free. She dropped the basket. Scrambling and sliding on
the mud, and grabbing at vegetation and rock to save
herself from falling, she continued on toward the wood.

She shuddered with cold and fear, yet tried to
reassure herself. Once in the wood, she would find
shelter and wait until somebody came for her. But they
should have been looking for her already.

She climbed on, her eyes directed on the ground,
wishing the moon would come out. Once it peeped out
from behind the clouds, only to disappear again. At
least the rain had slackened somewhat.

Finally she arrived on the edge of the wood. Huge
stones and boulders cluttered the slope, forming, she
fancied, a kind of wall around the grove. She scrambled
on farther into the wood, and realized that those
boulders seemed to be scattered all over the place.

Then the clouds parted and the moon shone fully on
this grove of ancient oaks. Beatrice gasped at the sight
she had certainly not been prepared for. In the eerie
light of the moon the dwarf oaks looked like fragments
of a dreadful nightmare. Or elements of a fairy tale that
had terrified her as a child.

Her eyes round with horror, she stared at the con-
torted, twisted limbs of the oaks. Never before had she
seen such misshapen trees. Cascades of moss and lichen
draped the crooked limbs, making them more terrifying
still. And thick underbrush hardly allowed one to see

the ground. Only the large boulders were discernible, themselves well overgrown with lichen and moss.

The cold night wind of the moors swayed the crooked branches and moaned and whistled around them, as if bemoaning their sad state. This wood was called the last of the primeval forest. "Primeval" is right, thought Beatrice, coming out of her terrified daze and trying to pull herself together. She was hardly surprised that Jean was afraid of this wood. It was a splendid setting for terrifying tales.

Beatrice shook off her momentary fear. It was a horrible place, but trees were trees, after all, and nothing to be afraid of. And she must find shelter. A large boulder from which a gnarled tree seemed to sprout, might give her some protection. She moved forward, stumbling and catching her dress on the thorny underbrush.

The rain had ceased, and the boulders and trees would give some shelter from the cold wind. She battled on. A small boulder, almost smothered by ferns, stood in her way. She would be obliged to clamber over it or go around it. Abruptly in the moonlight Beatrice noticed some faint round shape slithering across the stone. Light bands alternated with dark bands on its sinuous body. A viper! The thought leapt to her terror-stricken mind, and she screamed. She had disturbed a viper.

Viper! She had never thought of them, and nobody had mentioned them, but she should have known there would be snakes here. Paralyzed with fear, shaking with terror as much as with cold, she stood on the spot as if rooted to it, not able to move. What could she do? Where should she go?

Abruptly eerie laughter sounded in the woods some-where behind her. Beatrice's heart leapt with fright. She whirled around, stumbled on a stone, and with a loud cry fell headlong into the underbrush. The fall knocked the breath out of her, and she remained on the ground gasping and sobbing, hysteria threatening to overcome her. She fought for control, for composure. If she did not move, the snake would leave her alone, she hoped fervently. The eerie laughter must have been a bird.

But the laughter was repeated, and—Beatrice's eyes started from their sockets—a ghostly apparition seemed to float in the mist whirling about the trees. Beatrice's heart was pounding so hard it was choking her. Her throat was dry. It could not be a ghost, she tried to reassure herself.

She shut her eyes, and when she opened them the apparition had vanished. And so had the snake. But something was definitely moving in the underbrush. Twigs were creaking, branches swished, and something was moving toward her.

Beatrice wanted to scream, but was unable to utter a sound.

The rustle among the underbrush grew louder. Beatrice, unable to move, closed her eyes and prayed.

Abruptly something cold and wet pressed itself against her cheek. She gasped. Her eyes flew open. A cold wet nose was nudging her face and a tail was wagging furiously.

"Prince!" Beatrice cried out in relief. Squire Cavanaugh's dog. "Prince," she cried again, throwing her arms around the animal and hugging his soft furry shape. Thank God. Prince!

The dog gave a loud, friendly bark.

"Lady Brook!" From somewhere in that dreadful grove the squire's voice rang out, muffled by the swirling fog.

"Squire Cavanaugh, Squire Cavanaugh," cried Beatrice, as jumping to her feet and holding on to the dog, she started to tear her way toward the voice.

Fourteen

"You are an addlepated idiot, and I'm not apologizing for my words," Lord Brook was saying to his wife. "How could you allow yourself to fall asleep on the moor?"

He had just returned to Brook Manor and had barely changed his attire to a bottle-green coat and biscuit pantaloons when he discovered what had occurred and stormed into his wife's bedchamber.

Beatrice sat up in bed, indignant. "I did *not* fall asleep. I was drugged," she cried. The bedcovers had slipped, revealing her milk-white bosom, imperfectly concealed by her blue silk nightgown.

"Nonsense," countered his lordship. "You overtaxed yourself. Taking strenuous walks on the moor two days running is too much. You are not used to this. It is hardly surprising that you grew tired, and with the warm sun shining upon you, you fell asleep. You are lucky that you were only chilled. And if the squire hadn't happened to call on us and discover that you intended to visit him, and therefore gone to look for you, you would have been much worse off."

"But I never intended to call on him after going to Wistman's Wood," cried Beatrice in puzzlement. "I don't know *where* the servants got that notion."

"Well, you must have said something to the effect, or else they would have started looking for you in Wistman's Wood.

"Hell and the devil," he abruptly swore. "It seems I cannot leave the house for a few days without your landing in a scrape. What a wife I have saddled myself with."

Unbidden tears pricked at Beatrice's eyes. "It seems you made a bad bargain, my lord," she said, her voice husky with emotion. After all she had gone through, to be scolded by him was the last straw. It was not to be borne.

A hot tear rolled down her cheek, and Beatrice brushed it angrily away. "I shall try to be less of a burden to you in the future."

Another tear rolled down silently.

The baron took out his handkerchief and dabbed at her cheek. "Pray don't cry, Beatrice," he said, his tone suddenly gentle.

Beatrice gave a loud sniff. "I am not crying. Pray do not be afraid that I shall treat you to an exhibition of the vapors and hysterics. I know you dislike excessively such display of sensibility."

She gulped and raised her tearstained eyes.

Like dewdrops on a primrose, it suddenly flashed through the baron's mind. She was beautiful even when crying. Suddenly he felt a great tenderness for her and a great desire to cherish and protect her, as indeed he had vowed to do at the altar. *Then* those words had had no meaning for him.

He caught himself up short. What was he about? He could *not* be falling in love. With his own wife? How unfashionable. His lips curled in derision.

Beatrice, watching the play of emotion on his countenance, sought to divine his thoughts. For a moment she fancied she had read tenderness and caring —she did not dare label it "love." Then his face clouded again. She gave an inward sigh. "I don't as a rule allow myself to cry," she said. "I must be more overset than I thought." She blew her nose on his handkerchief. "Oh, I'm sorry. I shall have it washed," she said, looking at the crumpled ball in her hand.

"Forget it," he said roughly. The desire to hold her in his arms, which ran counter to all his reasoning, was not to be denied. "And I know you cannot help being overset. To be alone on the moor can be an unsettling experience."

Beatrice relaxed. The derisive look had gone from his face. But it was replaced by one that sent hot blood rushing to her cheeks. What an unpredictable man was her husband. As unpredictable and changeable as the moor itself.

Her heartbeat quickened. She strove for composure. "That dreadful Wistman's Wood," she said somewhat breathlessly, yet trying to sound quite conversational. "I have never seen anything so terrifying."

"Nonsense. It is not terrifying at all."

"What about that bloodcurdling laugh I heard?"

"A nightbird perhaps. There are often strange noises on the moor at night."

"Well, this was not on the open moor. This was in the wood. And it was no bird, it sounded quite human. And what about the apparition I saw?"

He looked at her half-pityingly, half in scorn.

"Very well, very well," said Beatrice testily. "Perhaps I only imagined it. Perhaps it was only moonlight playing tricks with those horrid trees. But I never wish to see that dreadful place again."

"I am disappointed in you, Beatrice. I would not have expected to hear this from you."

"But—"

"You saw it for the first time in the dark, during a storm, while you were afraid. I own that it must have seemed to you ugly and terrifying. But if you had seen it by daylight, you would have appreciated what a singular spot it is. I shall take you there when you recover. You must shed your prejudice against it, against Dartmoor. I shall make you love it as I do."

"Why?" she asked innocently, gazing up into his face, a provocative little smile playing upon her lips. She could not help herself. Could not help responding to the look in his eyes, to the attraction that seemed to emanate from him like a force that was trapping her in a delicious dream of forgetfulness. Forgetfulness of all save one thing.

"Why? You know damn well why." Suddenly he groaned. "Oh, hell and damnation. I want you, Beatrice."

His arms went about her and his lips pressed upon hers fiercely, hungrily. His hands tore imperatively at her nightgown.

Somewhere at the back of her mind, Beatrice had misgivings, but that faint doubting voice was unheeded as she responded to his kiss and embrace with all her pent-up feelings.

"Beatrice, Beatrice," he said huskily as his hands continued their task of disrobing.

"Oh, Gareth . . ." Beatrice felt as if under a spell. A delicious spell that made her whole body tingle with pleasure, made her unaware of everything but delight at each touch of his hand and his strong body.

And before he too forgot everything, the baron fleetingly thought: It doesn't matter now if the child succumbs to the fever. The succession shall be assured.

But it was not to be. Not today, at all events, for a sharp knock on the door rudely intruded on their privacy.

With an oath, the baron jerked away, while Beatrice, her cheeks scarlet, her heart pounding, hastily pulled the blanket up to her ears.

"Come in," she called out.

Mrs. Teswick, her countenance severe and hostile as ever, stood on the threshold. "A caller for you, my lord," she said tonelessly. "Waiting in the green saloon. Will you partake of supper in your chamber, ma'am?"

Beatrice, conscious of great annoyance and disappointment, and perhaps a dash of relief, said absently, "No, no. I daresay I shall be well enough to go down to supper. Who is the caller?" And as the housekeeper's brows rose, she added in the direction of her husband, "Or should I ask?"

"Why not?" he said irritably. "Who is it, Teswick?"

"Captain Tremblay."

"Oh. I shall be with him directly. Pray excuse me, Beatrice." He rose and bowed stiffly, straightening his disheveled attire. The familiar cold expression returned to his face. The fantasy was shattered. Reality in the guise of Mrs. Teswick had sobered them both.

Beatrice sighed with dissatisfaction and regret as the door shut on the housekeeper and her husband. What a pity, it struck her, that Teswick would come in just then, and she was surprised at her thought.

But she couldn't waste time on introspection or regret. The captain was here. Would he berate her husband again? His former threats loomed large anew in her mind.

She jumped out of bed and put on her pink silk dressing gown and slippers. She would go to the green saloon and pretend she wished to ask Gareth something, thus discovering at least whether their discussion was amiable or not. She had to know. After all, the captain *had* threatened Gareth once before. Gareth would not tell her what had occurred between them, and whom else could she ask?

At the door to the green saloon she hesitated. There was no need for her to go in, for though she could not distinguish the words, the voices within were raised in anger. This made an apprehensive Beatrice slowly retrace her steps. She could not just walk in and demand to know what it was all about. No matter how much she wished to know. In the corridor she met Edgar.

"Beatrice, what are you doing out of bed?" he cried, much astonished. "And in your . . . er, robe, too."

Beatrice flushed in vexation. "I wished to seek out Albinia, and I mistook the turn in the corridor. I still am not quite recovered."

He hurried forward and took her arm solicitously. "Of course you aren't. It is not to be wondered at. Pray allow me to lead you back to your chamber."

Beatrice permitted him to lead her along the corridor, wondering if she should confide to him her anxiety about her husband. Would he know about the quarrel between the captain and Gareth? And would he tell her?

So engrossed was she with her worrisome thoughts that she paid hardly any attention where she was going, and stumbled and stubbed her toe. But for Edgar's support, she would have fallen.

At that moment, as she leaned on him before straightening to resume her walk, loud steps pounded on the corridor, and Lord Brook turned the corner.

His countenance darkened as he beheld Beatrice, seemingly in Edgar's arms.

"Beatrice has not quite recovered yet," Edgar explained.

"On the contrary, I think she has recovered splendidly," said the baron. The icy contempt in his voice and the grim expression about his mouth sent a chill through Beatrice's heart.

Then he turned on his heel and marched out of their presence, leaving Beatrice so vexed she could cry. Surely Gareth could not think Edgar and she were doing something . . . improper?

Yet why was he suddenly so different. Or was it merely his dislike of his nephew transferring to Beatrice because she was in his company, without any suspicions of impropriety? Surely he could not think . . . ?

I ask only one thing of you—fidelity! The words rang in her mind like a bell. But surely he . . . She gasped. Why, it was absurd. And, she further thought with outrage, it was only her worry about him that had caused her to be out in the corridor. And Edgar had merely come upon her and helped her. That was all. Gareth could not suspect her or Edgar—his own nephew—of . . . No, no. She was surely imagining things.

That night Beatrice lay awake in bed listening for the sound of her husband's footsteps approaching her chamber. She watched and waited for a long time, but he did not come.

Fifteen

The next two days Beatrice found very unsatisfactory. The baron kept himself aloof, spending most of his time with his men of business or visiting his tenants' cottages on the moor. And Camilla's supercilious smile when she called at Brook Manor did nothing to improve Beatrice's spirits.

But the squire paid a call on Beatrice and brought her some beautiful marsh voilets and moor orchids. Albinia, thinking the bouquet was for her, stretched out her hand for the flowers. When the squire, ignoring her hand, presented the bouquet to Beatrice, a mortified flush stole into her cheeks, and an angry glitter showed in her eyes. Albinia might have resented the squire's frequent visits, but she clearly disliked his dancing attendance on Beatrice. In fact she was so incensed that she remarked angrily later that it seemed to her the squire was in a fair way of becoming Beatrice's cicisbeo —a remark Beatrice found quite absurd.

On the third day Lord Brook announced he would absent himself again from the manor.

"Where *are* you disappearing to so often?" Beatrice could not help exclaiming, biting her lip in vexation the moment she uttered the words. As a wife-in-name-only she had no right to pry into his business. Yet it annoyed her not to know.

"It has to do with my inheritance," he answered.

"You have seen the place—it needs much improvement. Grandfather had rather neglected it. No," he forestalled her, "you cannot come with me. I shall be obliged to travel to several places and I think—"

"I was *not* going to beg you to take me along, but you did promise to take me to Wistman's Wood."

He looked at her scornfully. "I thought you wished never to see it again."

Beatrice's cheeks turned pink. "I did, but . . . but I do wish to see it now, by daylight."

"Let Edgar take you," the baron said curtly in a harsh voice. "Or Sir Oliver, or even the captain."

"Perhaps you should also add the squire," cried Beatrice, nettled. "I wish to go with *you*."

"Why?" he asked, an unfathomable expression in his dark eyes.

"Why? Why? Because I wish to."

"Don't play with me, Beatrice," he cried.

"I am *not* playing. I wish to see if you were right about Wistman's Wood, and if you were, I . . . I thought you might like to witness me change my mind. Oh"—she threw up her hands—"if you dislike the notion now, let us just forget the whole thing."

"No, no, we shan't forget it. Can you be ready in half an hour?"

"Of course I can," said Beatrice, glad that he had agreed.

"The weather is perfect now, but it might change later," he added.

And in half an hour's time they set out for Wistman's Wood, Beatrice again in her sturdy boots and a serviceable skirt and spencer, Lord Brook in leather breeches and a blue coat.

But if Beatrice thought to recapture the baron's mood of two days ago, she was disappointed. For the most part he remained silent, only casting appraising glances at her from time to time. He was very attentive, helping her to cross the river by the stepping-stones and up the steep slope, but without much comment or any sign that he had given up his absurd notion that she encouraged Edgar's attentions. Only when they stood in the ancient oak grove did his stiff pose relax a little.

"Well, what do you think of Wistman's Wood now?" he asked, looking at her expectantly.

Beatrice was astounded. Whereas before the grove had appeared terrifying, a figment out of a horrible nightmare, now, in the light of a bright sunny day, it looked merely picturesque and pleasant. The gnarled, twisted trees, decorated with an abundance of moss, lichen, and fern, presented a singularly interesting appearance. The fresh green color of the leaves, with yellow and red showing here and there, and plants and flowers, invisible by night, gave the whole a cheerful appearance. Whortleberry bushes, growing at the foot of the trees, delighted the eye with their red bells. And a rabbit scuttled across the underbrush.

Beatrice took a deep breath. "You are right, Gareth," she said. "There is nothing sinister in the wood by daylight." But she frowned. There had been that specter . . . and the laugh. She must have imagined the specter, and the laugh was a nightbird. Beatrice dismissed them from her mind.

"Thank you for showing me how silly my fears and my dislike were," she said warmly.

He relaxed even more. "Would it tire you too much to climb to the tor?" he asked abruptly. "Do you wish to rest now?"

Beatrice's heart leapt with pleasure. "Just a short rest will suffice. Which tor do you have in mind? There are so many of them."

"Great Mis Tor has the best view. But others, like Longaford and Higher White, have good views also. And they are much closer."

They sat down on some boulders, and while they rested, the baron began to tell Beatrice the history of Dartmoor: the origins of those large granite outcroppings, the envolving presence of man on the moor since prehistoric times, the lore and legends of the region. And as he talked, his restraint and stiffness fell away from him completely and his eyes shone with enthusiasm and love for this desolate and wild place, which yet could show such haunting beauty, as Beatrice had already discovered for herself.

Beatrice found his tales fascinating, and even more so the man himself. His countenance was transformed and animated, showing great sincerity and warmth.

And then he took her to the tors. And on the way he made her aware of a wheatear flying across the moor, showed her its nest among the boulders, and pointed out and explained to her the various prehistoric sites along the way. Then he helped her to clamber up the tor. By now Beatrice was rather tired, but glancing anxiously at her husband, she observed that he seemed as fresh as when they had started out. He needn't worry about his old injuries, she thought with relief. It must be only sudden jerks, stepping the wrong way, or pulling a muscle that made them hurt.

The climb was well worth the effort, Beatrice concluded when she finally stood at the top of the huge granite outcropping.

The vast panorama of the moors stretched below and around her as far as the eye could see—hills and lush valleys, ribbons and dots of water, and many tors. And far in the distance she fancied she could even see Plymouth and the Sea. It was breathtaking. And hot also. Or perhaps she was only flushed with excitement. The breeze was cool, but not strong, and the sun was shining brightly from the blue sky.

They sat down on the warm rock. The baron put his arm around her and drew her close. "Isn't it magnificent?" he whispered huskily.

"It is," said Beatrice, twisting in his arms to look up into his face, her own countenance aglow with pleasure.

Her heart leapt as she gazed into his eyes. For she

read in them tenderness and . . . desire. And she welcomed that look. It was no use denying it. She was in a fair way of falling in love with her husband. She could hardly credit it, could not accept it as lasting, but while the feeling was there, why not enjoy it?

Abruptly a cloud marred his countenance. "That lily-livered, sneaking coward," he spat, thrusting her away from him. "For a moment I had forgotten." His voice sounded harsh and tortured.

"Edgar?" hazarded Beatrice.

He nodded grimly.

"Oh, Gareth, surely you're not back to that!" she cried with vexation. "I stumbled and he supported me. That was all. And the reason I stumbled was that I didn't pay attention to where I was going. I was overset because I heard you and the captain quarreling again. Oh, Gareth, why is he so angry? No, I know you don't wish to tell me. But pray do take care."

He was frowning and gazing at her searchingly. "You were eavesdropping—again," he accused her.

Beatrice tossed her head. "What if I was? I was concerned about you. And you would not tell me anything, and no one would, I'm sure. And I wished to know."

"It was most improper of you," he said, but his voice was less harsh and the thundercloud was clearing from his countenance. "What an inquisitive wife I have acquired. She must know everything, go everywhere. Well," he sighed in mock resignation, "I see I shall be obliged to show you around everywhere, so that you know what to guard against. Tomorrow I shall show you . . . Oh, I was going away tomorrow. Well, perhaps I can leave later in the day."

He gazed deep into her eyes. Then slowly his head lowered and his lips sought hers, at first gently, tenderly, then with ever greater insistence and passion as his hands tightened about her. And Beatrice responded with rapture and delight. Time seemed to stand still as they clung to each other, oblivious of all. Their passion seemed to be consuming them. Gareth's hands wandered over her body with even greater insistence. He began to unbutton her dress.

Beatrice, blushing and with pounding heart, realized what he was doing but was powerless to stop him. And in truth did not wish to. She had never known marriage could be such a delight. And then, he had hardly begun to disrobe her, when he tore himself away. The muscle at his jaw worked, his lips were tightly pressed.

Beatrice blinked, bewildered. "What-what . . . ? Why are you angry? What have I done?"

"Nothing. It is time we returned. I have some business to attend to. And you must be quite tired," he said in an expressionless tone. How *could* he be sure? How could he ever be sure? he thought grimly. "Shall I carry you part of the way? I would not want you to overtire yourself and become ill."

Conventional words uttered in a conventional polite manner. Beatice could have wept with frustration. His mood had changed again. She sighed. "Let us return," she agreed, hoping that tomorrow's excursion would have a more satisfactory end.

But the next day he took her onto the blanket bog of North Highland, and this setting was not conducive to a romantic interlude. The fringes of that enormous peat bog reached to within a few miles of Brook Manor, and Gareth wished her to be acquainted with walking in its dangerous places.

The peat bog was not one big morass, but was interspersed with many solid clumps of peat, upon which it was safe to stand. To traverse *this* bog, one was obliged to jump from one such peat hag to another, being careful not to slip or to fall short and land in the mire, whose depths varied and could be, toward the center of Cranmere Pool, very deep indeed.

It was quite a different way of proceeding, but Gareth told her he had crossed in that fashion all the way to Okehampton on the northern edge of Dartmoor. Apart from this mode of traveling, there were moor paths across the bog, which it was dangerous to stray from, especially at night.

Beatrice did not enjoy this walk as much as yesterday's, but she appreciated Gareth's wishing to show her all aspects of the moor.

It was after they returned home that Beatrice received some vexing intelligence. Her abigail told her that Mrs. Teswick had originated the notion that Beatrice intended to call on the squire after her walk to Wistman's Wood. On hearing this, Beatrice at once bristled with indignation and summoned the housekeeper to her chamber. Mrs. Teswick, stiff and hostile as always, asked in a cold prim voice what Lady Brook desired of her.

Beatrice could hardly contain her anger. "I desire to know why you set it about that I was to visit Squire Cavanaugh. I told nobody any such thing. You did it on purpose, so I should not be missed. And if the squire had not chanced to come by, I might have spent a whole night in Wistman's Wood, with God knows what consequences. Do you hate me so much that you wish me dead and do not hesitate to bring this about?"

The housekeeper's lips compressed tightly, but her eyes burned with defiance. She seemed to have difficulty controlling herself, for the pulse at her temple throbbed and her bosom rose and fell heavily. "I'm sure I do not know what you are talking about, my lady," she said in a toneless voice, in which agitation was imperfectly concealed. "I believed, as did the rest of the household, that you had gone to pay a call on the squire."

"Don't lie to me, Teswick," cried Beatrice, stamping her foot. "*You* set it about."

The housekeeper's eyes glittered dangerously. "And who told you I set it about, my lady?" she asked, her expression clearly boding that someone no good.

Beatrice opened her mouth, then shut it. She did not know *who* had told her abigail, but Teswick might

guess. "It is of no consequence. I know it was you. I'm
warning you, Mrs. Teswick, don't provoke me too much.
I know something about you that would give me a perfect
reason to dismiss you. I don't wish to do it, for much as I
dislike you and wish to be rid of you, I am mindful of your
age and of your long years of service at the manor."

For a moment, alarm crossed the housekeeper's features. Then she gave a slight bow. "I'm sure I appreciate
your ladyship's consideration"—her voice sounded
hollow—"even though I am quite at a loss what your
ladyship is alluding to. And I did not spread the tale about
your calling on the squire." Although fear lurked in her
features, hostility and stubbornness predominated.

Beatrice gave an impatient exclamation. Teswick
would never own to the truth, she realized.

She took a deep breath. "I know you did so,
however, no matter how much you might deny it. And I
give you fair warning: dislike me as much as you wish,
but do not—I repeat, do not—play a trick like that on
me again, or you shall regret it." Would Gareth believe
her word against the housekeeper's? she wondered. No,
he would not suspect Mrs. Teswick of something so
base. He would say it was just a misunderstanding on
Teswick's part, even if he learned that she had spread
the tale. "You may go now," Beatrice said.

The housekeeper bowed stiffly, lips compressed, eyes
glittering with hatred, and stalked out of the chamber.

A very unsatisfactory resolution, thought Beatrice.
She should have been more forceful with Teswick, she
should have . . . She gave in impatient sigh. Well, that
particular trick the housekeeper wouldn't repeat, at all
events. Beatrice would always tell somebody precisely
where she would be going and when she could be
expected to return. And what else could Teswick do to
her?

Beatrice was soon to find out what else—if indeed it
was the housekeeper who was responsible for the prank.

Sixteen

Beatrice went to dinner in no very amiable mood, but forced herself to appear unconcerned, not wishing to give rise to more gossip and speculation. This time Edgar was missing from the table, having been invited to dinner by a friend.

It was while they were dining that a loud barking by the window heralded the squire's approach. "Not again," moaned Albinia, rolling tragic eyes to the ceiling. "He cannot stay away from us."

As before, the dog leapt over the windowsill and the squire followed suit somewhat less gracefully. The dog wagged his tail and greeted everybody in turn, even Albinia, who shuddered when his cold, wet nose touched her hand.

"Squire, if you don't take that dog away at once, I shall have a spasm," she warned him in dramatic accents.

"Prince, heel," commanded the squire. "Truth to tell, it is about him that I called on you today." He turned to the baron. "Would you oblige me, Brook, by keeping Prince for me?"

"Not while I am here," said Albinia categorically.

"Oh, hush, Albinia. Prince won't hurt you," said the squire somewhat impatiently.

Albinia's jaw dropped in shock. "Don't you hush *me*, Squire Cavanaugh. How *dare* you treat me in this improper, uncivil manner."

"You can't expect me to formally address a female whose pigtails I have pulled and who let my frog loose." He took a seat at the table.

"Good God. Does *that* still rankle after all those years? Why do you wish us to keep Prince for you?" she asked abruptly, momentarily diverted.

"I am obliged to go away and I cannot take Prince with me. He likes to be active and roam the moor. I thought, Lady Brook, that you would take him with you on your rides or walks on the moor."

"I don't wish her going walking or riding on the moor. Not without me," protested the baron.

Beatrice, still seething with anger, instantly bristled at this. "I should very much like to take Prince along with me, Squire Cavanaugh. Now, Albinia, don't put yourself in a taking over a trifle. Prince can be kept in the kennels."

"He knows the moor better than I do," said the squire. "Even I might become disoriented in the fog, but not he. Good friend to have around."

"Roger, I wish you wouldn't put notions into Beatrice's head. She is not going on the moor alone."

"If you think that, m'boy, you don't know much about females," said the squire. "Not that I ever thought you did. If I know your wife, and I fancy I took good measure of her—no offense ma'am—she is not likely to stay away from the moor."

"I don't know what all the fuss is about," complained Beatrice. "I certainly don't wish to wind up in the bog again. I'll take precious care where I'm going, if I decide to go at all. Prince can get his exercise in the park. I would be delighted to walk with him."

"As long as you don't walk him into the house," said Albinia with some hostility. "There, just look, he tracked mud across the carpet. Oh, no," she wailed, "you did too, Roger. Roger Cavanaugh, you are the most exasperating man of my acquaintance."

"We must have stepped into a puddle in the yard. Not to worry, the domestics will clean it off. Tell me, Lady Brook, what would you think if I gave a party in your honor? Would you like the notion?"

"Why, of course I would," exclaimed Beatrice. "I don't even know where you live. I collect it must be quite close to Brook Manor."

"You never gave a party for *me,*" cried Albinia, displeased and piqued.

"You were never a newlywed," the squire answered. "Though you *could* have been." His eyes twinkled, but there was a pensive look in them too.

To Beatrice's astonishment Albinia colored up to the roots of her hair. "Roger, if you bring *that* up again I shall . . . I shall . . ."

"Drum your feet and have hysterics," supplied the squire, unrepentant. "I *know* you can do it. I've seen you."

"When I was ten years old. As if I would do anything so undignified as that," Albinia said, much affronted.

"No, I agree you would not. Not now. Now you would clutch at your bosom and moan, 'Oh, oh, I shall have a spasm. Ooh, where is my vinaigrette.' "

He did such a perfect imitation of Albinia that Beatrice was hard put to it not to giggle. The baron repressed a smile, but Albinia turned alarmingly purple, her eyes shooting daggers at the squire. She spluttered, but in her indignation words failed her.

The baron said, his voice a trifle shaky with mirth, "Take care, Roger, or you shall provoke an attack. And you know, with people her age one can never be sure if the malady is genuine or not. You would not want her death on your conscience."

Albinia choked at this sally, while Beatrice, eyes full of mirth, turned her face away from her sister-in-law.

Albinia threw down her napkin and rose majestically from her seat. "I shall not remain here and be insulted," she said. "I shall retire to my chamber." And she sailed out of the room, two red spots burning on her cheeks.

Once the door had shut behind her, Beatrice gave vent to her mirth. "You are a splendid mimic, squire. But weren't you a trifle hard on her?" Beatrice was pleasantly surprised at her husband also: he had shown a sense of humor and even was not above teasing his prim sister. "And you too, Gareth."

His countenance sobered. "I spoke only half in jest. She is probably healthy enough, but she can work herself into an illness if overset or provoked too much. And her indolent style of living is not at all conducive to good health. Dr. Maynard knows she dislikes walking, so he suggested Margate or Brighton. Or even the waters at Bath. But she won't hear of it."

"Well, if she had married *me,* she would be striding all over the moor now."

Beatrice's eyes grew round at this speech of the squire's. "Married you?" she cried, astonished. This time he did not seem to be jesting. "I beg your pardon, squire, but have you ever seriously contemplated marriage with Albinia?"

"Scores of times," the squire said cheerfully, and lowered his gaze to inspect a dish of food on the table.

Beatrice's jaw dropped.

"Roger offered for her . . . oh, a long time ago; but of course Father would not countenance his suit. A mere squire aspiring to a baron's daughter? Unthinkable." Gareth's lips curled in disdain.

"And Albinia never married!" exclaimed Beatrice involuntarily.

"If you think she's still wearing the willow for me, you're mistaken in the notion," said the squire. "Truth to tell, her other suitors bored her to death. They took all her megrims and whims at face value, and tolerated them all, instead of standing up to her. Of course they bored her. Now? Now"—he shrugged—"she is set in her ways. But if only she could be coaxed out-of-doors . . . See if you can persuade her to take a walk, Lady Brook."

"I shall try," said Beatrice dubiously. "But pray call me Beatrice. After these confidences, I think we can dispense with formality. Don't you think so, Gareth?"

He shrugged. "As you wish. You'd better place the dog in Jem's, the stableboy's care." He began to rise.

"I shall be happy to take the dog to the stables," offered Beatrice. "Where do you live, Roger?" she asked again.

"Northwest of here, as the crow flies. Cavanaugh Court. It's a longish way by road, but there is a shortcut across the moor. Let Brook show you." He rose also.

"I shall be leaving soon," said the baron. "Can I give you a lift?"

"Much obliged, m'boy. Good day to you, Beatrice. Take good care of Prince. And Albinia." His left eye closed in a conspiratorial wink.

Her husband took his leave of Beatrice also, and a moment later the two men left the chamber.

Beatrice remained alone with Prince, who, when commanded by the squire to remain, reluctantly flopped at her feet.

Beatrice fondled his silky ear. "We shall take a walk on the moor as soon as I can get my breath back," she said. "With you by my side, what shall I fear?"

Beatrice thought she would spend the rest of the day quietly in her chamber or keeping company with Albinia in the drawing room. But Albinia, not very good company in the best of times, declared herself unwell and kept to her chamber, emerging only for a brief moment to see Camilla, who came to pay a call on her.

Camilla had promised to fetch her a book, but she had forgotten to bring it along, and promised to return with it later in the evening.

Beatrice went up to her chamber and lay down, but very soon discovered she was too restless to sleep, unsettling thoughts dashing back and forth through her mind. At last she was forced to conclude that it would be of no use to stay there. She would take Prince for a short walk. Perhaps that would divert her mind. She rose, put on her gray walking dress, spencer, and boots, called Prince, and started for the moor. Before leaving, however, she informed the butler where she was going and directed him to send a groom looking for her if she did not return within two hours.

She was pleased to discover from Pedmore that Alice was showing some improvement. Then, on an impulse, she asked, "Does Mrs. Teswick have trouble with her eyes?"

"Ah. You have found dust on the furniture," he said. His starchy face showed perturbation for a moment. "I shall see that it does not occur again." He spread his hands. "Yes, her eyes are failing her, and the maids know it and don't do their work properly. I scold them, but I don't wish to tell her or she would turn them off or punish them severely. I don't wish for that. She has always been very strict, but since her eyes have been failing her, she's becoming even worse. What shall your ladyship do? I beg your pardon. It is not my place to ask."

Beatrice was pleased. The butler was unbending and seemed to have shed his dislike of her.

"I shall do nothing. For the present I shall bide my time. Don't tell her that I know. And don't worry, I shan't fly into a pet if I find dust on the furniture again. But tomorrow come to my chamber. Make a list of the servants' names and duties. If I see something done wrong, I shall speak directly to the person responsible."

"Very good, my lady. I'm sure your ladyship will treat everyone with justice and compassion. Even Teswick."

He cleared his throat.

"Pray accept my apologies," he said in a wooden voice, his countenance an expressionless mask. "We all wished for Miss Camilla to be the future Lady Brook. It was understood. But it was wrong in us to show it. To show our disapproval. I beg your pardon."

Beatrice smiled up at him. "I accept your apologies. And you, least of all, showed your dislike. Like the perfect butler you are. I'm glad you no longer feel hostile toward me. I should like us to get on well."

"I shall do my poor best to please your ladyship," said Pedmore, visibly moved.

Beatrice felt cheered by this encounter with the butler, glad that the servants were beginning to accept her for what she was, not as a person who had ousted Camilla from her rightful role. She had not tried to run the household and was treading slowly, except in those instances where Teswick's cruelty or insulting conduct provoked her anger.

With an almost jaunty step she set out on her walk, Prince trotting at her side, his tail wagging.

Seventeen

Beatrice was just cutting across the heather, having left the path, the dog bounding ahead of her, when she heard horses' hooves approaching, and glancing back, noticed two riders cantering her way along the road. Beatrice frowned. She recognized Camilla's riding habit, and the man in the officer's uniform must be the captain. She grimaced and increased her stride. Camilla had returned, as promised, with the book for Albinia.

Beatrice heaved a sigh. The sight of Camilla acted as a damper on her senses. Yet she should not allow the mere sight of the former betrothed of her husband to overset her to such an extent. Oh, if only one could turn off one's feelings at will, she thought wryly, and forged ahead among the heather and gorse bushes, but very mindful of the emerald patches on the moor.

The sound of the horses' hooves grew louder; then—she blinked—some hoofbeats began to recede, while some were drawing nearer.

She whirled around. The captain was galloping toward her.

He saluted smartly as he caught up with her. "Good evening, Lady Brook. I am delighted to see you again." He dismounted, unconcerned about his horse, and bowed low over her hand. "Pray allow me to spend a few moments in your company." As he came up from his bow, Beatrice's nose informed her that he must

128

have been refreshing himself quite liberally with brandy.

Beatrice sighed, her suspicions of the captain leaping to her mind. "I cannot forbid you to walk on the moor," she said rather ungraciously, "but I wish to be alone."

"You are overset, and quite naturally so, because your boorish husband has absented himself again. And so soon after the wedding ceremony. He does not appreciate you as he ought. But what can one expect from someone who has treated my sister so shabbily?" He scowled.

"I cannot believe that Gareth has behaved improperly," cried Beatrice. "What is he supposed to have done?"

"Ah, he did not confide in you. Well, I gave him my word I should keep my counsel for a short while longer, to allow him to do justice to my sister. But if he does not act soon . . ."

Beatrice was dismayed. "I can assure you that whatever it is, my husband shall do the honorable thing."

"So I would have expected from him. But it is nearly a year since Waterloo and my sister still lives in the shadows. Oh, if only I had been aware of the whole at the outset. But I was away soldiering, haven't seen her, only on short furloughs, if at all. I did not know what had occurred, did not know of the child."

"Child? Whose child?"

"Why, my sister's, of course."

"And who . . . who is the father of the child?" Beatrice asked, her heart giving an uncomfortable leap.

"Whom do you fancy it to be, Lady Brook?" he countered with an enigmatic smile.

Oh, no, no. It cannot be, thought Beatrice. She owned the notion had occurred to her before, only to be pushed resolutely aside. And yet, why not? This sort of thing happened not infrequently. Had the captain's sister been Gareth's mistress and had he cast her off without providing for her properly? And what had the Battle of Waterloo to do with it, unless it was a soldier's way of marking time. "I'm sure I have no notion," she said coldly.

He gave her a searching look. "I think you have a very definite notion, and I should enlighten you. But I shan't. Lord Brook has overset us both, so why don't we console each other?"

Beatrice stiffened. His speech was a trifle slurred, but the gleam in his eye was quite easy to comprehend.

He took her arm and drew her close. He was quite foxed and obviously in an amorous mood. Beatrice grew apprehensive. In his state he would not likely listen to reason. "Have you not come with Camilla?" she asked. "And has she not gone to the manor? You should not have deserted her."

"Camilla can fend for herself. It's *you* who need an escort. Oh, yes, you should not be walking alone on the moor, my lady. You never know what might occur." His grip on her arm tightened.

Beatrice tried to free herself. "Pray let me go, sir. Pray recollect yourself. You are a gentleman. And I am Lord Brook's wife."

"Perhaps you shall soon be his widow," he said, striking terror into Beatrice's heart. He bent his head, making her feel nauseated with his hot brandy-laden breath.

If he tries to kiss me, I shall scream, thought Beatrice. But who shall hear me here? "Pray let me go," she cried, twisting her head away from him.

Abruptly loud excited barking startled them both. Prince, Beatrice thought with relief. She had forgotten him. He had streaked off across the moor and become lost to view among the boulders.

The captain swore. "What the devil is the squire's dog doing here?"

"He came with me."

The dog was barking, jumping up the captain's immaculately clad legs, leaving smudges of mud and dirt on his boots and breeches.

"The devil," swore the captain. "Down, down, you beast. Look at my breeches. Take yourself off." He glanced with dislike at the mud stains on his clothes, then threw up his hands. "I shall take it out of your hide one day," he said threateningly to the dog.

Prince snarled.

Disregarding the dog, Captain Tremblay tried to take Beatrice in his arms. She fought him off. "You are foxed. You don't know what you're doing. Pray let me go." Her cries became mixed with Prince's barking as he jumped between them and up the captain's leg.

"Get away, get away, you meddler, you dumb animal," cried the captain. He gave the dog a strong cuff. And the dog, now angry, retaliated by sinking his teeth into the captain's hand. "Oww," cried the captain, stepping back, and stumbled on a stone and went over backward into heather and muddy soil. The dog stood over him, teeth bared, ready to attack again.

"Prince, Prince, stop it. Call him off. Damnation, you know me, Prince."

"Prince, heel," commanded Beatrice. "I think you had better go," she said to the captain, "while your horse has not yet bolted. Prince shall protect me, if I tell him to. And when you're sober, you shall thank Prince for putting a stop to your most improper advances."

The captain picked himself up, swearing, jumped onto his horse, and rode off with a darkling look at the dog and a bow to Beatrice.

Whether the fall had brought Captain Tremblay to his senses, Beatrice was not sure, but she decided to return at once to the manor. She did not wish to chance his changing his mind, even with Prince by her side. With heaving bosom and rather disheveled attire she reached Brook Manor. Just as she was entering the yard, she saw Camilla and the captain ride off. The captain apparently had had his attire cleaned, and seemed to have sobered somewhat, for as he came abreast of her he bent over and said in a low voice, "Pray accept my apologies, Lady Brook. I was not myself today."

She nodded her head coldly. "As long as your behavior shan't be repeated."

"It shan't be repeated," he said fervently.

"What shan't be repeated?" Beatrice had not noticed that Edgar had come to stand by her side.

"The captain was foxed and he forgot himself on the moor." Edgar's brows drew together in anger. "Do you ever get foxed, Edgar?"

He shook his head. "Not since I was up at Oxford. It gave me a headache I don't care to experience again."

"I am glad of it. People who are foxed can be unpredictable in their conduct. And I should like to know that you at least shall always be the same."

"Of course I shall always be the same, always dedicated to your service," he said with fervor.

Beatrice frowned. Then her countenance cleared. After all, there was no harm in Edgar's admiring her. And it was good for her spirits.

"Edgar," she abruptly asked, "do you know why the captain and my husband are at odds?"

His face lengthened. "I was hoping you would not discover it. But I suppose it was inevitable. I shouldn't have thought the fellow would mention it to you, inebriated or not. But you should not refine too much on it. Men *will* have these little affairs, although one might think he would have left her well provided for. I don't see what else the captain could be aggrieved about. Surely he cannot expect Uncle to marry his sister, when he is married to you."

Then Edgar did not know of the child, it suddenly struck Beatrice.

"Are you taking Prince to the kennels?" Edgar asked. "May I walk with you? I had intended to tell you later what has happened, but you might hear the gossip from your maid and be concerned."

Alarm crossed Beatrice's features. "What has occurred? Is it something to do with Mrs. Teswick again?"

He nodded.

"That woman."

"Pray don't put yourself in a taking. I have seen to everything."

"But what?"

"It's about Alice, the maid. Mrs. Teswick wished to return her to her old duties. Knowing you would not wish it, I took it upon myself to remonstrate with her and prevailed upon her to allow the woman to regain her full strength first."

"Oh, Edgar, I am so grateful to you," cried Beatrice warmly, pressing his hand.

He returned the pressure. "Anything to be of service to you, Beatrice," he said with great sincerity. "Shall I take Prince to the kennels for you?"

"No, I wish to look in on Arrow, my horse."

"Shall I see you at supper?"

"I'm not sure. I am not very hungry."

"Then if I don't see you tonight, have a good rest and a peaceful night's sleep." And he bowed and walked off rather hurriedly toward the manor.

What a good friend he was, Beatrice reflected as she crossed the yard. He did not linger or intrude on her with his company, even though he would plainly have wished to. It was only later that the uncharitable thought occurred to her that he hastened within because night was slipping her dark mantle over the moors and the manor.

Beatrice left the dog in Jem's care, visited Arrow, and made her way to the house rather more tired than she cared to admit. Disquieted by the encounter with the captain, she was pondering over her husband's strange conduct. Did he treat all females with such callous disregard? Would he wind up hurting her also?

So sunk in pensive thoughts was she that she became aware of Prince padding quietly beside her only when she was going up to her chamber by way of the back stairway.

"Prince, what are you doing here?" she asked. He must have slipped out and followed her, she thought. Well, she was *not* going back with him. She would ring from her chamber for someone to fetch him. "Well, come on, now, you shall pay a visit to my bedchamber," she said, fondling his silken ear.

The dog nuzzled her and wagged his tail. And padded along with her up the stairs.

A branched candlestick was lit brightly, and Beatrice's bed was ready to receive her, but the coverlet was not turned back, which was something her maid usually did before nighttime. Yet Beatrice's slippers and nightgown were laid out. She called on her abigail, but Collins did not answer. Beatrice looked into the dressing room, but the maid was not there. Oh well, she had probably gone to fetch some tea, thinking Beatrice might wish to refresh herself upon her return.

Suddenly she became aware of the dog's steady growling. "What is it, Prince?" she called out, and reentered the bedchamber.

The dog was standing by the bed, baring his teeth, and the fur on his back bristled.

"Wrrrr, wrrr, wrrrr," Prince growled, advancing on the bed as if on a foe.

"Now what? What's the matter, Prince?" she asked, puzzled and suddenly apprehensive. She stared intently at the bed. Was it her fancy, or did something move under the cover on the bed? Her heart leapt up in fright.

She approached the bed.

Prince gave her a warning bark. Then another.

Beatrice, heart pounding, grabbed at the corner of the cover and flipped it over. And drew back in horror.

There, coiled at the foot of the bed, was a black-and-white snake. A viper. Disturbed, it now began to slither across the bed.

Beatrice froze. Rooted to the spot, unable to move, she watched helplessly as the snake slowly made its way toward her.

Eighteen

Prince began to bark excitedly, jumped toward the snake, then jumped back, and repeated the maneuver several times.

Beatrice came out of her trance. If only she had a stout stick handy, she thought. She glanced around desperately for a weapon. Prince was teasing the snake with his barking. The thought flitted through Beatrice's mind that if Albinia heard him, shd would have a spasm.

Abruptly a sharp knock sounded on the door, and Beatrice slumped in relief. "Come in," she called out in a quavering voice.

"Prince? I thought it was he. What is he—?" Edgar, in the process of shutting the door, broke off as he beheld the tableau: Beatrice, petrified, staring at the bed; the snake crawling toward her; the excited barking dog.

"Stay where you are. Don't move a muscle," Edgar cried. "Prince, stay away from it." He backed out of the room. Beatrice could hear his footsteps pounding on the corridor.

He was back in a trice, carrying a pistol. The snake had slid off the bed and was now crawling toward Beatrice. But the dog had placed himself between it and her and kept growling and barking at it. "Prince, heel," commanded Edgar while he took aim.

The sound of the pistol shot reverberated in the air, and the snake collapsed lifelessly on the floor.

"Oh, Edgar, Edgar," sobbed Beatrice with relief, but still quite shaken and in the grip of terror, "if you hadn't come, if Prince had not alerted me, I would have crawled in between the sheets and . . . and would have been killed by it. Oh, Edgar . . ." No longer able to control herself, Beatrice burst into hysterical sobbing.

With two steps Edgar was beside her. "It is well . . . everything is well now. You no longer need to be afraid," he soothed.

But Beatrice, quite shaken and overwrought, threw herself at him and clung to him, sobbing and shuddering, unable to control herself. This last incident was just one too many for her.

Edgar gathered her to himself and stroked her silken black hair and murmured soothing words, trying to calm her.

Abruptly Beatrice's startled abigail, a tea tray in her hand, burst into the room. "What is going on—? My lady!" She recoiled in horror as she beheld the snake on the floor and Prince nuzzling Beatrice's leg.

"Take it away quickly. It is dead," said Edgar. "And take the dog away too. Now, go. He'll go with you. Just take him before Miss Risborough hears his barking and we have *her* hysterics on our hands."

"But . . . but how—?"

"Oh," sobbed Beatrice, "where were you, Collins?"

The abigail placed the tea tray on the side table. "That dratted Teswick kept me in the kitchen, prosing on how I should conduct myself. So I gave her a piece of my mind. I am not her servant. How—?"

"Never mind the questions," Edgar said tersely. "Just take that thing away. Don't be afraid to touch it. It is quite dead. Pick it up with a napkin if you're loath to touch it with your bare hands. Your mistress is unharmed, just shaken. And quite naturally so."

The abigail, with a shudder, carried out his orders.

Beatrice's sobbing was abating somewhat. Edgar was

still holding her close. She was quite pale and shaken by the incident, but now she could ponder over the matter. "Who could have done it?" She gulped, looking up to his face.

"It was wrong, very wrong," said Edgar, shaking his head. "Whoever did this to you—it was most unjust. Your being Uncle Gareth's wife is not your fault. I mean, it isn't as if you had set your cap at him or . . . or anything. And you had no notion he had been affianced to Ca—" He broke off, reddening.

"Oh, you needn't stop. I know of that. I only wish I had known it at the outset. I wouldn't have been so puzzled why everyone here dislikes me so."

"Ah, no, no, not 'dislikes,' " cried Edgar. "No one could dislike you, Beatrice, who has been more than a few moments in your company."

Beatrice groped for a handkerchief in the reticule hanging at her waist. He pulled his own out, and she blew her nose. The abigail had gone with the dead snake and the dog, and Beatrice, no longer obliged to see the dead serpent, was regaining her composure. "Do you think it was Teswick?" she asked, watching his face.

"I don't know." Then, "It had to be," he said in a somewhat disjointed manner. "But it is wrong, all wrong."

"I couldn't agree more that it is wrong," a cold, cutting voice suddenly interrupted, startling them both and causing them to spring apart. "But you should have thought of that *before* you took my wife in your arms."

"Gareth!" said Beatrice, aghast.

"Yes, Gareth. I came a trifle too soon for you," he said with a curling lip. He was livid with rage as he came forward into the room.

"No, no. You're quite mistaken. It is *not* what you think," Beatrice cried.

"So I am mistaken, am I, you jade."

"Uncle Gareth—"

"Silence!" the baron thundered. "I shall deal with you later. I half-suspected something of the sort. I turned back, wishing to surprise you, Beatrice. For the pleasure of it, I told myself. But what I really wished was to lay my doubts to rest. I should have known better. And I should have known Edgar would be up to his—"

"No, Uncle Gareth, no. You don't know what has occurred."

"Gareth, pray let me explain," Beatrice begged.

"I don't need any explanations. The evidence of my own eyes is quite sufficient." He turned on his heel and strode out of the room, his limp quite pronounced.

"He is limping. He must have hurt himself," Beatrice cried. But she cried to empty space, for the door had shut behind him.

Beatrice started forward. "I must go to him. I must explain."

Edgar placed a restraining hand on her arm. "Not now. He is in a black rage. No telling what he might do."

"You . . . you don't think he might become violent?"

"No, no, of course not," Edgar said quickly. Too quickly and vehemently. "But his temper since Wa . . . since he sustained his injuries can be unpredictable sometimes, and he flies into a passion. Pray let his temper cool."

"What if he goes riding or walking on the moor? It's dangerous when one—"

"He won't go tonight. What you should do is to take some laudanum and get some sleep. In the morning you will be able to deal with everything much more effectively."

Beatrice sighed. "I suppose you're in the right of it. But how could he accuse me . . . us?"

"Obviously he does not realize your true nature. Doesn't realize that base emotions can never find a place in your heart. Oh, Beatrice, Beatrice, if only I had met you sooner. No, no, pray do not say anything. I beg your pardon. That slipped out. Take the laudanum— Oh, good,'' he added as the door opened to admit a much-shocked and pale Collins. ''Your mistress needs a good night's rest and to compose herself after this shock. Some laudanum would be in order.''

''But I don't wish—'' Beatrice started to protest.

''Of course, directly,'' said the maid, a spark of anger in her eyes. ''What I wish to know is, how did an adder get into Miss Beatrice's bechamber? Surely it could not have crawled here by itself. I know, that witch Teswick!'' she abrupt y cried. ''My lady, you must turn her off. It must be her—''

Edgar put up a hand. ''Now, that's enough. Conjectures can wait until tomorrow. Put your mistress to bed now.'' He turned and possessed himself of Beatrice's hands. ''Pray don't dwell on it, Beatrice. And don't worry, I shall have a word with Teswick. If it was she who did this, I shall make sure it is never repeated. That woman is ready for Bedlam,'' he added more to himself than to her. He released Beatrice's hands and turned to go.

''Edgar, how shall I ever repay you for saving my life?''

His smile was a little twisted. ''I wish I could tell you how. But since I can't, you will please me by forgetting all about this unpleasant incident.''

''How *can* I forget it? She meant to kill me, Edgar.''

''Or merely to frighten you.''

''But it could have killed me. Oh, Edgar—''

''Now, Beatrice, pray don't start working yourself up again.'' He glanced meaningfully at the abigail.

She nodded in understanding.

''Good night, Beatrice, and pray don't worry. This shall not be repeated, I assure you.''

And he went out of the chamber, leaving Beatrice in a perfectly distracted state.

To the shock of discovery of the snake was now added the strong dismay at her husband's mistaken notion that she had been cuckolding him with Edgar. She wished so much to set him straight on it at once. But Edgar was right: she should wait until tomorrow.

Tomorrow, when it came, however, presented her with a fresh problem. When she finally awakened late from her drugged sleep, she discovered that Gareth had left the house on foot, intending to go to Devil's Tor and then on to Cranmere. And he probably planned to be on the moor all day, since he had taken a small basket of provisions with him.

Cranmere—the worse peat bog in the Dartmoor Uplands! Beatrice could well understand why he had gone there. He needed the physical exertion and the solitude of moor to assuage his pain. If only he had waited a trifle longer. If only *she* had not taken the laudanum. If only . . .

With feverish haste Beatrice dressed, put on her walking dress and her sturdy boots, and, mindful of the bog, provided herself with a stout stick and a rope, then fetched Prince and set out across the moor.

Her groom wished to go with her, but she declined his escort. She wished to be alone with Gareth. Even the presence of a servant would make it more difficult for her to persuade him to the truth. She looked forward to this task with a heavy heart and apprehension, having doubts as to her ability to persuade him that she had not played him false.

Why should it be so important to her, she wondered as she strode along, when her marriage was only one of convenience? She heaved a sigh. It has ceased to be one of convenience only. She cared about Gareth, cared what he thought of her, although she still could not think she was really in love with him. She could not believe *that*. But regardless, she must convince her husband of the error of his belief. And she must convince him before his rage made him do something imprudent, like not paying attention to where he was going. Rage could make one blind to one's surroundings, and as he had told her himself, on the moor danger lurked for the unwary.

She increased her pace. She must catch up with him in time to prevent an accident.

Unfortunately, she was to catch up with him just a trifle too late.

It was about noon when the baron halted on a slightly larger mound of peat to refresh himself, having no notion that his wife had started out after him. Bitter and disgusted with himelf after a sleepless night full of torment and jealous rage, he had sought the solace of the moors, which always brought him some measure of composure. Not this time. He was physically tired from the arduous walk, but his mental anguish had not diminished.

He had no wish to eat. The mere sight of food nauseated him. But the bottle of wine he greeted with relief. He drank long and deeply, even though the wine tasted bitter. Everything turned to bitterness for him now, he reflected, his lips twisting painfully.

When he finished, he rose and resumed his walk. But for some reason, he found the quivering peat hags much harder to negotiate now. Surely he couldn't have become inebriated, even though he had drunk the wine on an empty stomach. But he hardly made the next jump, he was so unsteady on his feet. A dreadful suspicion suddenly leapt to his mind. Followed by an even more heartrending one.

He took another jump—and missed. He fell headlong into the black morass. That had never happened to him before. Even with his injuries, he had remained sure-footed. His dreadful suspicion was now confirmed in his mind. *Both* his suspicions were confirmed.

He floundered in the bog, trying to reach the peat hag to haul himself up. But a great lassitude overcame him. His body refused to obey the commands of his mind. She had drugged him, the jade, he thought, his mouth full of ashes. She had put laudanum in his wine to get rid of him. So she could marry Edgar. Edgar . . .

His arms were sliding back into the mud. His eyes were closing. "Beatrice," he groaned weakly in despair. Beatrice, you treacherous witch.

He was up to his waist in the bog. His senses were becoming clouded, confused. The black peat bog was claiming him as its own. Up above, a raven croaked, as if confirming his doom. But he heard only *her* voice, saw only *her* lovely body cradled in the arms of his nephew.

Beatrice . . .

Nineteen

The sun was high in the heavens when Beatrice, almost exhausted, called a halt and sat down carefully on a peat hag to rest her weary limbs. And still she had not caught up with her husband. He must have been driven by rage, to have traversed this distance without stopping. She believed she would have caught up with him, had he stopped to partake of the food he had brought along.

Beatrice now wished she had brought some food also, for she was quite hungry and some nourishment would revive her strength. Prince stood beside her, wagging his tail and panting a little, but he was in much better shape than she. Beatrice stared at the desolate brown undulating expanse of the moor, trying to discern her husband's tall figure.

"Where is he?" she asked the dog. "Prince, you tell me. You take me to him. Perhaps he is just on the other side of that hump. We must go on, or I shall never catch up with him before nighttime."

She shuddered. Never again would she be caught at night on the moor. And what if the fog rolled in? Fortunately she now knew that the season for long-lasting fog was over. The mist, even if it came in, should dissipate reasonably soon. For were she caught in the mist, she would not venture one step farther.

She sighed, fondling the dog's silky head, and rose. "Come, Prince. He *must* stop and partake of some

nourishment soon, and then, if we can catch up with
him, he'll share it with us.''

The dog barked as if in anticipation of the meal, and
jumped ahead of her to another hag. Beatrice picked up
the stick and rope and marched on. Only somebody
born and bred on the moor would find *this* locomotion
easy, she reflected. One's muscles must be used to that
endless jumping from one firm spot to another.

"Firm" was a relative description for the quaking
mounds of peat, but at least one did not sink waist-deep
into the black mud and water that separated them.

The sun kept on shining. The trill of a curlew was the
only thing that interrupted the silence on the moor. That
and, far away, the gurgle of a stream as it made its way
from the uplands, where it was born, into the lush valley
it gave life to.

Beatrice crested a peat hill. Prince, who had tarried
behind, diverted by some creature, now bounded
forward and suddenly, on reaching Beatrice, became
quite excited, jumping and barking and twirling around
her legs.

"You'll fall off the hag if you keep this up," Beatrice
admonished him, but her heartbeat quickened. Had he
scented Gareth?

She scanned the brown, muddy horizon but could not
see her husband's tall figure striding along anywhere.
She sighed. "Go ahead, Prince. Lead on," she said, and
was surprised to see the dog veering to the left.

But that's *not* toward Cranmere, she thought in
dismay. That's veering off the route. Had she become
disoriented, or had her husband changed his direction in
midstream? Or . . . Her brow furrowed. He was going
to Devil's Tor first. And that would be somewhere to
the left. She followed Prince, but could see nobody
jumping from peat mound to peat mound. Yet the dog
was bounding eagerly forward without hesitation, and
she followed suit, calling out breathlessly after him,

"Wait . . . wait, Prince. Not so fast. I am not a rabbit."

Where was Gareth? Abruptly, as she lowered her sight to the ground to follow the dog's progress, she saw something that made her gasp and stand still, frozen for a moment.

There, in the bog by a peat hag, immersed in the black ooze, was a person, a man. Gareth? It had to be. But. . . Her heart hammered with fright. He was not trying to scramble to firm ground, was not moving, not even floundering.

Holding up her skirts, the rope coiled over her shoulder, the stick under her arm, she jumped nimbly from peat hag to peat hag, suddenly finding the strength and skill to negotiate the bog faster and easier than before.

It *was* Gareth. "Gareth, Gareth . . ." she cried.

But there was no response. Only a further sliding of the body into the mud.

Body? Was he perhaps unconscious? Terrified half out of her wits, Beatrice kept jumping toward her husband and calling out his name. But it was Prince's barking that seemed to rouse him at last. Prince was now standing on the peat hag above him, and his bark reverberated in the stillness of the moor.

The figure in the mud moved, one arm lifted weakly, only to fall back in.

Beatrice jumped, slipped, swayed, regained her balance, and raced on. His shoulders and head were still sticking out of the morass, but for how long? Heart pounding, breath coming in painful gasps, throat dry, Beatrice rushed on.

It seemed like an eternity before she stood on the peat hag beside which her husband was mired. "Gareth," she cried, dropping to her knees and stretching out her hand to grasp his arm. Prince was still dancing on the spot and barking, but Gareth was not attempting to save himself. His eyes were closed and his arms had slid into the mud.

"Gareth," Beatrice cried, panic-stricken. "Gareth, give me your arm. I can't reach you, and I'm afraid I shall overbalance if I try."

His eyelids flew open. Black eyes full of pain stared at her, at first uncomprehending. "Go away, don't torment me," he muttered.

He is delirious. He thinks I am a ghost, Beatrice thought.

"It's me, Beatrice." She fell flat on her stomach, pushed herself forward, and reached out, trying to grab his shoulder. But she couldn't. "Gareth, help me. I can't pull you up by myself."

A glimmer of understanding showed in the half-closed eyes. "So you have . . . changed your . . . mind," he gasped out. His lips curled cynically. "But you have come . . . too late." The eyelids fell shut.

"Gareth!" Beatrice screamed.

The rope, the stick. She pushed the stick to him. "Grab at the stick. Oh, my God, Gareth, wake up." What was the matter with him? Was he injured? If only she could grasp his arm . . .

"Gareth, take the stick. Gareth!" She must not lose her composure. She must remain calm. The rope—if she could get the rope around him . . . "Gareth, help me," she cried as panic threatened to overcome her. Her teeth chattered with cold.

Gareth's eyelids fluttered open. "Help? You need *my* help?" With supreme effort, it seemed, and agonizingly slowly, his arms lifted out of the mud.

"Grab the stick," Beatrice shouted. And his mud-coated hands closed around the stick. Thank God. She began to pull.

But his hand was slipping. The rope! "Put the rope around you," she cried, making a loop of the rope and throwing it to him. Perhaps the bog wasn't very deep in this spot, she prayed, panic-stricken.

Gareth contrived to thrust his arms through the loop,

and Beatrice had just enough time to tighten the rope around him before his eyes shut again.

"No, no. Gareth, wake up. You must scramble onto the hag." She began to pull on the rope, but his body, heavy with mud, was difficult to move. "Gareth," she shrieked.

He opened his eyes and stirred.

"Come on. You must get out of the mire. Prince, help me to pull him." She thrust the rope at the dog's muzzle, and he grabbed it.

"Gareth, try."

Whether the dog helped her, Beatrice wasn't sure, but somehow she contrived to pull Gareth close enough to the peat hag so that she could grasp his arm. Then she was straining to drag him onto the hag. He made a strong effort to help her, and managed with her aid to push his arms and shoulders onto the peat mound. Then suddenly he went limp, his eyes shut.

"Gareth," Beatrice cried.

He did not respond.

My God, is he dead? she thought, cold despair gripping her heart. But his stertorous breathing proved he was not dead. He was asleep—at worst, unconscious.

She pulled at his limp body. She mustn't let him slide back into the mud, or she'd never be able to haul him up. "Prince, grab him. Help me pull him up. Stop jumping up and down like a puppet and stop that dreadful barking. Help me to pull. Quick, before he slides back into the mud. Grab his coat."

Panting from her effort, perspiration blinding her eyes, Beatrice contrived, with some help from the dog, to pull Gareth all the way out onto the peat hag and out of the mud that clung tenaciously to his body. Throughout all this, he remained oblivious. Was he drunk? His breath smelled of alcohol. But what folly, to drink oneself insensible on the moor. He must have taken leave of his senses. Yes, just as he had taken leave of his senses to suspect her and Edgar of cuckolding him. Edgar, his own nephew. And she—did he have so little trust . . . ?

How *could* he suspect her of being so base? Her terrible fear for his life had been replaced by an over-whelming relief. And after relief paradoxically came anger at his subjecting them both to such an ordeal. She could have boxed his ears, she was so vexed with him. Instead she cradled his head on her lap as she sat on the peat hag lovingly wiping the mud from his face. There was not much room on that peat tuft, just enough to hold them both and the dog.

In repose Gareth's countenance looked younger, less severe, and more vulnerable. Beatrice's heart grew cold at the thought of his near escape from death. If he had died . . . She bit her lip. It seemed impossible that she could have fallen in love with him. She had never thought she would, after Roderick, yet now she could think quite dispassionately about her former love. It was the present man in her life—her husband—who stirred such deep feelings in her.

It was doubtful those feelings would last, but for the moment Beatrice's heart had no doubt at all. Yet, he did not love her. He was attracted to her, yes, and naturally he wished her to be faithful to him, but true love . . . And what of the captain's sister, who had borne his child? Beatrice was now sure that Gareth had absented himself from the manor to call on her. That was why he did not wish to take his wife along. Did he love this ineligible woman? For she must be ineligible, else he would have married her.

She shook her head impatiently. Pondering this wouldn't get them out of the present fix. Who knew how long he might remain in this stupor, and if the weather changed and it began to rain . . . She wasn't even sure he would be able to walk. She dared not leave him to go for help, for in his stupor he might slide back into the morass. Prince must go home and fetch help. But how was she to send the message that she needed help?

The handkerchief, her monogrammed silk handkerchief, stained with the peat-bog mud, and . . . and the baron's stick pin.

Quickly she removed the stickpin and thrust it through her handkerchief and secured it to Prince's neck.

"Prince, go home," she commanded. Surely he would know how to return home.

The dog looked at her and cocked his head. She pointed in the direction she thought the squire's home was located. It should be closer than Brook Manor. "Go home, Prince. Home."

He barked but refused to go, looking at her expectantly.

"No, I can't go with you. I dare not leave Gareth. Now, go quickly. Before the weather changes. Go home."

The dog still did not move, his intelligent eyes gazing questioningly at her.

"Go home," Beatrice repeated in a sharp, irritated tone.

And Prince, as if hurt at her anger, turned and jumped to the nearest peat hag. The next moment he was running, bounding across the bog without hesitation, as if he knew exactly which way to go. And he probably did. On his ramblings with the squire he must have taken that route dozens of times.

Beatrice hoped the squire's people would deduce what had occurred. After all, they must know where the squire had left his dog, must recognize the stickpin. The squire . . . Only now it dawned on Beatrice that the squire had purposely left his dog at Brook Manor as a protection for her, for surely one of his servants could have walked the dog on the moor. She was surprised she hadn't tumbled to it sooner. A warm rush of gratitude welled up within her. The squire was concerned for her welfare, just as Edgar was.

She stared at her unconscious husband and her heart contracted. To some he might not be handsome, but to her his was the dearest countenance on earth. Even though relaxed in sleep, the lines of pain were still here. She wished she had not been the cause of his pain. But he had brought it on himself with his jumping to conclusions.

You have changed your mind. She abruptly recalled his words. Changed her mind about what? And too late for what? Well, she had been almost too late to save him, she conceded that, but she had never been of a different mind about wishing to explain to him about her and Edgar. If he had allowed her that explanation last night, this would not have occurred. Instead he had gone out on the moor and drunk himself into a stupor.

She hoped he would come out of it soon, but he remained obstinately asleep. Even when the squire's men and the grooms from Brook Manor arrived, he did not waken. The men had quite a time carrying him out of the bog, but apparently they knew where it was safe to go, for even if they sank up to their waists, they kept his body aloft and contrived to get him out of the bog without mishap. Throughout all this, Prince kept barking excitedly and jumping up Beatrice's legs, making it more difficult for her to negotiate the peat hags.

But at last they were off the bog and returned to the manor. Gareth was tenderly carried to his chamber, where his valet fussed over him, while Beatrice's own abigail did the same for her. The commotion brought on another of Albinia's spasms, although Beatrice, beyond telling her that she had found Gareth asleep on the moor when she caught up with him, did not confide to her the whole.

Albinia put her own interpretation on the event. "I've never seen Brook taken up to his chamber in an inebriated state," she said querulously. "And it's your fault that he is in that deplorable condition. I have rarely seen him so cross as he was this morning. Depend upon it, it's because he is vexed with you for encouraging the squire's advances."

"What? Pray don't be so absurd. I'm not encouraging the squire's advances, and he is not making any."

"Well," cried Albinia, much outraged, "if fetching you flowers and leaving that dreadful dog of his here so you can have company on your walks is not making advances, I should like to know what is. It has been ages since he brought *me* any flowers. Nor does he ever think *I* might wish company."

"But, Albinia," Beatrice protested between laughter and exasperation, "you hate Prince. As for the squire's company, you say that it makes you ill."

"That's neither here nor there," said Albinia in a petulant voice. "The fact remains that Squire Cavanaugh has never so much as looked at another woman, much less begun courting her, but he does both with you. I'm not surprised Brook has been provoked to anger."

"How can he court me, when I am married already?" But Beatrice realized it would be useless to argue, so she fled to her chamber to take a bath and fret over Gareth's continued state of unconsciousness. If one did not know better, one would think he was drugged, she reflected.

Her observation was justified when at last Gareth awakened and she, disregarding the protests of her maid and his valet, went to his chamber to have a heart-to-heart talk with him.

He was propped up on pillows, looking pale and weary and extremely cross.

Beatrice was a trifle apprehensive, but chasing the

valet away, she perched on her husband's bed. The heavy purple velvet curtains on the windows were drawn, and only a candle illuminated the gloomy chamber, the massive oak four-poster with the deep purple curtains, and the dark oak wainscoting and the tapestries on the walls.

"Your valet tells me you have suffered no ill effects from your fall on the moor, and I'm glad of it," she said, puzzling over the hostile look that sprang to his eyes at her words. "I wish to speak with you, Gareth," she continued. "That's why I followed you on the moor. You may not recall it—"

He laughed unpleasantly. "Oh, yes, I recall it," he said grimly. "You changed your mind. But if you came to apologize—"

"Apologize? *Apologize?*" Beatrice frowned in annoyance. She had not expected a warm show of gratitude for having saved his life, but this . . . "I have nothing to apologize for. You were quite wrong about Edgar and me. If you had but given me a chance to explain—"

"Oh, yes. Explain and be damned. No, don't trouble yourself to deny what my own eyes have seen. I did not expect you to apologize for *that*, though God knows you should. No, I expected you to apologize for trying to kill me."

"What? Are you out of your senses, Gareth? You must be," Beatrice cried, stunned, hurt, and astounded at this statement.

"Aye, you may well stare. You almost finished me off there on the moor. I suppose I should be grateful to you for changing your mind. I'm not sure if I am, though I should be gratified that at least, as things stand now, you are not a murderess."

Beatrice stamped her foot, sparks of wrath in her deep blue eyes. "Gareth, pray explain yourself, for I have no notion what you are talking about. What is this insane babble about my wishing to kill you? Whatever gave you such an idea?''

His lips curled sardonically. "Oh, that is good . . . upon my word, it's good," he said with heavy sarcasm, his burning dark eyes expressing his contempt. "But you shan't convince me, madam, with your playacting."

"You *are* ready for Bedlam. When have I tried to kill you?"

"When you put laudanum in the wine, hoping I would become drugged, fall into the bog, and drown."

"What!" Beatrice suddenly felt weak. And she was sure she had paled. "So the wine was drugged," she said in a hollow voice. "I own the thought had crossed my mind. Oh, not about the wine, but about your unnatural stupor. But . . . but who could have done it?"

"You, madam wife. To get rid of me so you could marry Edgar." His words were dripping with bitterness.

"Oh, you are insulting and provoking," Beatrice cried, and jumped up from the bed, the sparks of warth in her eyes flaming into a raging fire. "How dare you accuse me of such dastardly action? You have no reason to suppose so."

"No?" he said ironically, an unpleasant curl to his lip. "I would say that catching you in your bedchamber in Edgar's arms was reason enough."

"But you don't know what had occurred. There is a perfectly innocent explanation for what you saw."

"Pray don't try to tell me that you stumbled again and he rushed all the way to your chamber to support you. No, no, you cannot make me believe that."

"How can I make you believe anything, when you don't allow me the chance to explain?"

"I am not interested in your explanations, in your *lies,*" he abruptly lashed out at her. "Lies and deceit. And I, fool that I was—I was halfway to falling in love with you."

He gave a mirthless laugh, full of self-derision. "Fool that I was, I allowed myself to be beguiled by your lovely face and figure and . . . and what I thought was your admirable character."

Beatrice's heart was pounding. The revelations he had just made and the accusations he had hurled at her made her head spin. The knowledge that he had been falling in love with her made her breathless, but his unjust accusations made her furiously angry. And her outrage overbore any other consideration.

"Well, I am very grateful that your eyes have been opened at last. For I'd rather have that snake love me than you," she spat at him. "And I can only be grateful that things"—her cheeks colored up—"that things with us have not progressed to a greater intimacy, which I would have infinitely regretted." Her bosom was heaving. "I hate you, Gareth, I hate you from the bottom of my heart. And I rue the day that I agreed to marry you. I shall never forgive you for this, never. I shall always hate you, and if I could revoke my marriage vows, I would do so at once."

"You forget one little detail," he said unpleasantly. "If you divorced me, what would happen to your papa's debts?"

"I don't care. I don't care anymore. They forced me to marry you, and I was prepared to make that sacrifice. But I had *not* bargained on your character. Now I can comprehend why Ev . . . why some people find you so revolting. For I do too. I wish you were dead."

All blood abruptly drained from his countenance. And from hers. A short silence followed, which hung between them like a grim dividing curtain. Gareth's white lips were tightly pressed.

"Gareth, Gareth, I did not mean it. I didn't," Beatrice said in a small strangled voice. "But you provoked me so. My God, do you really think I wished you dead, when I jumped from one of those accursed peat hags to another till my legs ached and I was well nigh to dropping from exhaustion? Was it from hate, do you think, or a wish to see you dead? Or was it because my heart was breaking at the thought that you might have become careless and fallen into the bog? And when I saw you lying there in the morass, I had never known such panic and grief. Oh, Gareth, Gareth.''

For a moment something like dawning joy lit up his eyes. Then his countenance hardened. ''Lies, all lies,'' he said harshly. ''I shall never believe what you say. You have drugged me.''

''I didn't. I . . . But who did? Are you quite sure you were drugged?''

''Oh, I was drugged right enough, and you know it.''

''Who could have done it?'' Beatrice puzzled, momentarily diverted. ''This is dreadful. You must inform the magistrate.''

He laughed unpleasantly. ''I don't wish for any more scandal.''

''But who . . . ? Oh, the captain, of course. He swore he would kill you.''

''*He* never meant it. Besides, poison is not a soldier's way of putting a period to a man's existence. It has a woman's touch. A dagger or a pistol would have been more to *his* taste. But why am I wasting my breath?''

''If it wasn't the captain, it must be Teswick. I am persuaded she had drugged *me*. And don't look so contemptuous and disbelieving. I was drugged on the day I went to Wistman's Wood.''

''You were overtired and fell asleep,'' Gareth said stubbornly, but for a moment he seemed to be quite struck by the notion. ''And even if she had drugged you, she would not have done that to me. She wouldn't have tried to kill me. Not unless she became a complete lunatic.''

''Well, I suspected her of being halfway to Bedlam at the outset,'' Beatrice said.

"No, no. I shall talk to her, but . . . What reason does she have to kill me? You, on the other hand"—his lip twisted with contempt—"you have a very good reason. Two reasons—my fortune and Edgar. Yes, it was you who poisoned me. And no amount of lying will make me believe otherwise."

"Gareth—"

A knock on the door interrupted her. The door opened to reveal the apprehensive countenance of Gareth's valet and the concerned face of Dr. Maynard.

"I beg your pardon, your lordship, but I took the liberty of fetching the doctor," the valet said.

Beatrice rose in a stately manner, though her bosom was heaving as she could hardly talk for breathless anger.

"Be sure you examine his lordship's head, Dr. Maynard. He is definitely queer in his attic. I shouldn't wonder if you declare him ready for Bedlam," she said, and stalked out of the chamber, her head held high, her cheeks two bright red spots, her hands tightly clenched.

That insensible, odious, cruel, contemptible man. And she had thought she was in love with him. Never, never, never would she fall into that mistake again. Never would she speak a word to him. Not as long as she lived. She would be obliged to remain with him until she could be sure all her father's debts were paid, mortifying though the thought was, but after that she would leave him. And if it took her the rest of her days, somehow she would contrive to pay that dreadful man every penny he had spent on her family.

Her rage at him was choking her. She hated him, hated him with all her being, and was only glad her eyes had been opened to his perfidy in time.

But if she hated him and did not wish to speak to or see him ever again, why was she so dreadfully miserable, so hopelessly hurt?

Fool, imbecile that she was, of course she was hurt.

That was only natural after what he had just said to her. She should be thankful that he had opened her eyes to his true character.

But she could not be thankful, berate herself as she might. She only felt a great sense of loss, an emptiness and an ache, the kind she felt when she had parted from Roderick for the last time and again when she had heard of his death.

Only, strangely enough, the present sense of loss was even greater and harder to bear.

She rushed to her bedchamber, threw herself on her bed, and, her composure having quite deserted her, burst into overwrought sobbing.

Twenty

Beatrice stayed in her chamber the rest of the day. She refused all the food and drink that her worried abigail offered her, refused to admit Dr. Maynard to her room. Yet perversely she sent the maid out to discover from the doctor the state of her husband's health. In spite of all, she wished to know. In spite of all, she cared, though her heart was breaking. And she worried that whoever had tried to kill Gareth might try again.

She asked her maid to fetch Edgar to her, then sent her out of the room. He had not been in the house when the squire's men came rushing to Brook Manor to alert the staff that their master must have had an accident on the moor, and he was still absent by the time Beatrice and the baron were rescued. But apparently Albinia or the servants had told him of what had occurred, for he looked quite shocked and concerned when he appeared before her.

"Beatrice, I am so glad that you are none the worse for your terrible ordeal. Nor, I am told, is Uncle Gareth. I infinitely regret that I was not here to come to your aid."

He looked positively ill, and his hand, when he touched her, was trembling. "It was such a shock to me. Pedmore told me of the situation. Apparently it was Squire Cavanaugh's dog that saved you both."

"Yes, Edgar, but I'm sure you don't know the whole.

Gareth claims he was drugged, poisoned with laudanum so that he would lose his footing and fall in the bog and die. And he . . . he . . ." She was choking over the words. "He thinks *I* did it, that I attempted to kill him because . . . because of you."

Edgar gave an impatient exclamation of disgust. "I thought he had given up that ridiculous notion about us."

"Well, he hasn't. Oh, he was most abusive. I never wish to speak to him again. But . . . but, Edgar, who could have poisoned him? I fancied at first that it was the captain."

Edgar pondered for a moment. "I don't think he would become so vengeful. He talks, yes, but it's just talk."

"Well, if not he, then it's Mrs. Teswick. And if that is the case, she must be insane and I don't wish her on the premises."

"I cannot believe it," Edgar said. "Did you tell Uncle of your suspicions?"

"I did, but it made no odds to him. He still thinks *I* did it," she said bitterly.

"Well, it's of no use trying to disabuse him of that notion for the present. Allow him some time to come to his senses."

"Oh, I don't wish to talk to him anymore. I was never so hurt in my life. But I don't wish the killer to remain undiscovered. It frightens me to have him roaming free. And if it's Teswick, who's to say that she won't burn the whole house, with us in it? I feel like fetching a constable and having her arrested, or having Dr. Maynard certify her and packing her off to Bedlam."

"Don't do anything rash," Edgar said quickly. "Pray allow *me* to investigate the matter first."

"Yes, but you assured me Teswick wouldn't continue to play her tricks. And now this follows so soon upon the snake incident."

"The snake—yes, she could have done that. But I don't think she would wish to harm my uncle."

"That's what Gareth said."

"Pray do not perturb yourself. Have your abigail sleep in your chamber, if you so desire, and don't go out on the moor alone. But don't do anything else—let *me* deal with this first. I shall do my utmost to discover the truth. I shall check on the captain, but—"

"Well, for my money, Teswick is still the most likely candidate. And she frightens me."

"I assure you, Beatrice, most solemnly, you have nothing to fear from Teswick from now on. I shall see to it. I don't wish you hurt. Do you think I wish a hair of your head harmed?" he suddenly exploded with passion. Then he caught himself. "Pray forgive me. I must go now. Pray do not worry. You are quite safe at Brook Manor." And he bowed and walked out of the chamber, leaving Beatrice just as overwrought as she had been before he came in.

If she was a trifle reassured about a potential killer roaming the house, her hurt and disgust with her husband had not diminished. And she felt very blue-deviled indeed. But toward evening, as she cried herself out, she became more calm and fiercely resolute to overcome her weakness and her sense of loss. Besides, she had known Gareth for a very short time. There was hardly time for her to have formed a lasting attachment. Her pride was hurt more than her heart.

Her words were echoed in another chamber, where behind the purple curtains her husband lay upon the pillows trying to persuade himself of the same notion, trying to shut out the memory of his lips upon hers and the feel of her body in his arms, hoping the bitterness of his dreadful discovery would in time erase that memory from his mind.

And in another chamber Albinia, hearing of the violent quarrel between her brother and his wife, though not the reason behind it, blamed Beatrice for encouraging the squire. And most of all she blamed Roger Cavanaugh himself. And hoped fervently she would never see his face again, or so she tried to persuade herself as she waited impatiently to see what—and whom—the next day would bring.

The next morning brought the squire. Cheerful and unconcerned as ever, he clambered over the windowsill of the dining room, with Prince at his side.

Albinia took one look and shrieked, "Get that dog out of here, Squire Cavanaugh." But Beatrice observed that the color had mounted to her cheeks. "Who let him out of the kennels?" She turned to Beatrice.

" 'Morning, Beatrice . . . 'morning, Albinia." The squire doffed his hat. "I let him out. As soon as I crossed the yard, he became so excited that there was no holding him. Besides, he was driving poor Jem to distraction with his barking. Down, Prince."

"Your habit of allowing your dog inside the house is most reprehensible," Albinia said icily, while regarding the primroses in his hand with a speculative eye and a quick glance at Beatrice. *Now* she did not presume the flowers were meant for her.

The squire bowed and presented the bouquet to Beatrice with a flourish. "For you, Beatrice. Picked them myself this morning by the Dart. I am happy to see you in good health after yesterday's adventure. And I'm glad Prince was of help to you both."

"Indeed yes," cried Beatrice warmly. "I am exceedingly grateful to you for your thoughtfulness in lending Prince to me."

"Always glad to oblige," the squire said. "May I have breakfast with you?"

He went to the sideboard and helped himself to the food and carried his plate to the table. After seating himself, he asked, "Brook is still keeping to his chamber?"

Beatrice nodded. "But he is feeling better. So his valet told me."

The squire's eyes roamed about the room. "And where is Edgar?"

Albinia shrugged. "Gone to Oliver's, I expect. As usual. He breakfasted early."

The squire speared a piece of cold beef on his fork and waved it at Beatrice. "Recall that little matter of a party I was going to give you, Beatrice? That's all arranged now. You shall receive a formal invitation, and you too, Albinia." He nodded carelessly in her direction. "But I should like to tell you I've changed the date. It's the day after tomorrow."

"What!" cried Albinia, much outraged. "Squire Cavanaugh, if you think one day's notice is adequate, you have windmills in your head. How can I get ready in one day? I shall need a new gown."

"You have scores of gowns in your wardrobe, Albinia. Wear the pink silk gown with the flounces. It's my favorite," he said, closing his right eye in a roguish wink.

"As if I would put on a gown to please you," cried Albinia, affronted.

Beatrice, wishing to forestall an altercation, said quickly, "The day after tomorrow would be satisfactory, though I'm not sure if it will suit your other guests."

"Won't be many guests," he said. "Just a few. You and Brook and Albinia. Oliver and Camilla and the captain, and yes, the parson to add respectability, plus a few others whom I'm sure you must have met at the church. But I have engaged an orchestra in case somebody should care for dancing."

"You don't have a ballroom at Cavanaugh Court," said Albinia, pursing her lips, but interest sparkling in her eyes.

Beatrice glanced from one to the other. If anyone

were the right man for Albinia, it was the squire, she
reflected wryly. He would know how to handle her
vapors and spasms.

"I have a ballroom *now*," said the squire. "I have
been renovating the whole place. You'll be surprised at
the changes I have wrought. You should like them."

Albinia shrugged. "I'm sure I don't know why," she
said pettishly.

"Then this is all settled, Beatrice? You'll come?"

"Of course. But I cannot answer for my husband."

"Dr. Maynard assured me Brook is well enough to
attend. And Edgar, of course."

After a few more pleasantries, and having finished his
breakfast, the squire took his leave of them; but not
before Beatrice was struck by a notion: she would tell
the squire everything—about Gareth, the snake, and
Gareth's accusations. She could trust Roger not to
betray her confidences.

But she would speak to him in private. She had
intended to tell Albinia this morning about the snake
incident and her suspicions of Teswick, but now she
decided it would not be the right moment. Albinia
would turn the whole house upside down, ordering the
servants to search for snakes hidden in the rooms. Also
Beatrice doubted she could be made to believe that Teswick had played this trick. Edgar had promised to look
into the matter, so Beatrice could safely talk to Albinia
about this *after* the squire's party. In any case, she was
sure Roger would offer her much better advice and help
than Albinia.

On the pretext of wishing to take Prince back to the
kennels—the squire still wanted her to keep the dog—
Beatrice accompanied Roger out-of-doors. Her need to
talk to him outweighed incurring Albinia's displeasure
at her act.

Once they were slowly crossing the yard and Beatrice
was certain they would not be overheard, she poured
out her troubles and suspicions to the squire.

He heard her out in silence, only posing a question here and there. When she had finished, he said, "This is a bad business indeed. But no need to lose your sleep over it. Just don't go out alone anywhere, and partake only of food the others eat."

"But if Teswick—"

"She wouldn't have attempted to kill Brook, not she."

"But if not Teswick, then who?"

Squire Cavanaugh looked pensive. "That is for us to find out."

"How?"

"Well, we shall contrive a way."

"How can we be sure that somebody won't try to kill him again? I shall take all precautions, but he won't."

"I'll try to impress upon him the necessity of doing so."

"I wish you would. But I have my doubts. Trying to impress anything upon my husband is a fruitless task. He is so set in his notions and beliefs that nothing can change him," she added bitterly.

"I don't think he so lost to all reason as you think. He is a bitter man, and with good cause. He has had much to bear in the last year. You must allow that those injuries inflicted upon him at Waterloo would have broken a lesser man's spirit completely. He has recovered amazingly well. If he but—"

"Waterloo? Waterloo?" Beatrice's eyes were round with surprise and wonder. She grabbed the squire by the arm and stared searchingly into his face.

"Of course Waterloo. But then, you know. You said you knew."

"Yes, I . . . I meant I knew he had injuries inflicted in a fight. Edgar . . . Edgar said it was a fight to end all fights."

"And so it was."

"Of course it was. Waterloo . . . But I . . . I somehow received the impression . . . I must have jumped to the wrong conclusion that it was a vulgar fight, a brawl or a duel. Edgar said Gareth did not wish to talk about it."

"Indeed not. But I collect you do not know why."

She nodded, bewildered. *"Now* I don't know. I fancied it was because he was ashamed of it. But . . . but it must be to the contrary."

"Oh, yes. He distinguished himself splendidly. And was honored for it. But his cousin—I suppose you did know he had a cousin."

"I only know of Edgar and Albinia."

"Percy was the son of Brook's uncle. But he was more than a cousin to Brook. He was also his best friend, and he died in the Battle of Waterloo, leaving a young wife. Expired in Gareth's arms, with his last breath begging Gareth to look after his young widow. *That* affected Brook deeply. His own wounds, the horrors he experienced, even, I suspect, the battle itself, meant little to him in the face of this deep loss."

"Ohh." Beatrice's eyes softened. "How I wronged him, thinking his injuries were sustained in an ignominious way. I wish I could tell him how dreadfully sorry I am to hear of his tragic loss."

"I wouldn't attempt it now. Not until the air is cleared between you two."

"But how can it be, when he still believes I poisoned him?"

"You leave that to me. I shall set him straight on that."

"Oh, would you, Roger?"

"Of course I shall do it. I think you are the right woman for him, Beatrice. And I think that deep down within him he knows it too. Perhaps the party will give him the opportunity to own it openly to himself."

Twenty One

It appeared at first that Lord Brook would not attend the squire's party. He came down to dinner, morose and uninterested in any projects of a lighter nature.

Albinia, quite convinced that the squire and Beatrice were "becoming lovers," seemed scarcely surprised that her brother and his wife behaved with icy formality to each other, and, herself vexed at Beatrice, was none too agreeable a dinner companion. If it weren't for Edgar, the atmosphere would have become strained indeed. Yet Beatrice with her newfound knowledge about her husband could not help feeling a trifle less angry toward him. But she did not attempt persuading him to attend the squire's party.

It was when Edgar, though surprised at the squire's plan, offered to be the ladies' escort to the party that the baron declared *he* would be coming also. Naturally, thought Beatrice with a curling lip. He still suspected them both.

Suspicions he might have, but at least he had tried to discover an alternative poisoner, as he told Beatrice, to her surprise, when he caught up with her in the hall after dinner.

"I just want you to know," he said stiffly, "that I talked to Teswick. And she categorically denies having poisoned me."

"Naturally she would," Beatrice said, her eyes full of

scorn. "You didn't expect her to admit it, did you?"

"No, but I fancy I could discern if she were lying."

"Just as you could discern that I am a liar," Beatrice said, thrusting out her chin. "I don't have much faith in your powers of observation, Gareth."

He scowled. "You don't have much faith in anything I say or do," he snapped.

"*You* can say that?" Beatrice cried, outraged. "Do you have faith in anything *I* say?"

He seemed nonplussed for a moment. He opened his mouth to speak, but at that moment Edgar joined them in the hall. "Uncle Gareth, I wished . . . Oh, I beg your pardon. I shall talk to you later," he said, discomfited.

"No need. I'm going up to my chamber," said Beatrice in a huff. "I suppose I should at least thank you for talking to Teswick," she said grudgingly to Gareth. "Much good it did you or anybody else. Good night, my lord, Edgar." And giving them a small bow, she swept out of their presence.

Nothing would be of any use—Gareth would never believe her innocent, Beatrice thought in despair, and immediately berated herself. Why should she care a button what he thought? She hated him, had only contempt for him. Why should his disbelief cast her in flat despair? But it was no use. She could not whip up enough anger against him to deaden her pain. Squire Cavanaugh's picture of the wounded, grieving hero leapt to her mind. Her heart contracted. Oh, how she could feel for him in his loss. Hadn't she herself suffered a like loss? If only he had shown that he believed her just a trifle.

But perhaps he did. Perhaps his questioning Teswick . . . Beatrice threw up her hands. Her own feelings toward him were so mixed—love and hate, concern and outrage vied for supremacy in her heart. She did not know anymore if she still loved him. If indeed she had ever loved him. After all, she had fancied herself in love before and thought it would be a lasting passion.

Of one thing only she was sure: her concern for his safety, his welfare, was real. *That* was not to be denied. She only hoped the squire's counsel would prevail and Gareth would take care to guard himself against the unknown assailant. And she hoped the squire's party would bring about some change in her relationship with her husband.

But the day of the party did not begin very auspiciously. A cold wind was blowing from the moors, a faint drizzle was falling, and wreaths of mist rose in the air. Albinia, who had wanted to travel in an open carriage, decided on the chaise, not wishing to ruin her splendid pink gown. Yes, she wore a pink silk gown with flounces, though she strongly asserted to Beatrice it was not done to please the squire, but because it was the most suitable one for the occassion.

Beatrice chose to wear her gown of emerald-green silk, of a deceptively simple cut, but with low décolletage and tiny puff sleeves, adorned with seed pearls. A green gold-spangled ribbon was threaded through her shiny black hair, which was gathered into a knot at the top, and an emerald necklace, an engagement present from Gareth, adorned her milk-white bosom and graceful slender neck. With the gown she wore gold slippers and long white gloves, gold reticule and light green gold-rimmed cloak. She thought the ensemble was adequate. Edgar thought she looked magnificent. Even her husband, who had not seen this particular gown before, could not conceal his approval of her looks. Only Albinia said she did not favor this particular shade of green.

Gareth himself, though not very interested in the party, did justice to the occasion with his attire. Resplendent in a sapphire-blue coat and drab-colored breeches, a sapphire stickpin in his snowy white cravat, he compared quite favorably with Edgar. Edgar, elegant in his dark green coat and biscuit-colored breeches, appeared to Beatrice, for some reason, like a handsome mannequin beside the striking figure of her husband. And in *her* eyes Gareth was definitely the handsomer of the two.

When they set out, the sky was completely overcast and it was raining, but they contrived to make reasonably good time without any mishaps, until they had traveled more than half the distance. Then an old tree, weakened by the storm, crashed across the road a few moments after they had passed the spot. They were not harmed, though shaken by the crash, and Albinia worried a trifle that the road back would be cut off. She was cheered, however, when shortly before their arrival at Cavanaugh Court the rain ceased and the sun peeped from behind the clouds.

The squire's house was a surprise to Beatrice. While it was built of moor stone, she realized it must have been extensively renovated, for it presented a lovely Palladian facade with portico and wide steps leading up to it.

Albinia's jaw dropped with surprise. "Well, I never," she gasped. "Compared to what it looked like, this is a palace. You must have spent a fortune on it, Roger."

The squire gave her a wide grin. "I knew it would impress you. That's why I had it done. Fit for a baron's daughter and sister. I'm sure you would feel right at home here."

"Squire Cavanaugh—" began Albinia, her eyes snapping with outrage.

The squire grimaced. "Now we are back to 'Squire Cavanaugh.' And I had hoped it would be only 'Roger' from now on."

He had come out himself to greet them, and never had Beatrice seen him so elegant. A maroon velvet coat, pale gray satin breeches, and his stiff cravat was as intricately tied as her husband's.

"You look splendid, Roger," she could not help exclaiming. "A fitting host to such an abode."

"And not a whiff of the stables," said the squire with a wicked grin at Albinia.

Albinia had the grace to redden.

"But come in, come in. My footmen's hands are getting sore from holding the doors open for so long." He waved them inside. "I don't as a rule greet my guests on the front porch," he explained to Beatrice, "but I wished to have the pleasure of watching Albinia's face when she caught sight of the house."

"She was quite impressed. And so am I," said Beatrice.

Albinia was impressed not only with the house but also with its master. She fairly devoured the squire with her eyes. And indeed he looked splendid in his finery.

Inside, the house was extensively redecorated, the squire explained to them as he proudly conducted them through the various chambers, ending up with the ballroom, where the musicians were tuning their instruments. This was a large cream-and-gold chamber with many tall windows and gleaming mirrors and glittering chandeliers. Designed by Adam, it was very elegant indeed. The French windows opened onto the terrace that ran along both sides and the back of the house. The house itself was situated on the edge of the moor, facing the undulating heather-covered expanse. On the left, sheltered by the house, was a small pleasant garden with a gazebo in its center.

In the garden and on the terrace chairs and tables were arranged for the guests. Colored lanterns decorated the shrubbery and the terrace, giving the grounds a very festive appearance.

The squire set his domestics to dry the chairs and tables, though the ground was a trifle too soggy for the ladies' delicate slippers.

"It shall dry out in no time," he said, undaunted by this minor setback.

The tour of the house completed, he led them back to

the drawing room, where the guests who had arrived before them had assembled. It was just as he had said: Dr. Maynard, the parson, Camilla, Sir Oliver and the captain, the local magistrate and his wife, and some other couples, all of whom Beatrice recalled having met at the church. The only guest who had not arrived was some particular friend of Gareth's who now apparently would not be able to come because of the blocked road, thus putting Gareth quite out of humor.

Having decided it would be of no use to wait any longer for this last guest, the squire gave the sign for dinner to be served, and they all filed into the dining room.

Apparently the squire had not related the incident of the snake to Gareth, nor had Edgar, or Gareth would have mentioned it to Beatrice. Only Albinia had heard via the servants' gossip that a snake had crawled into Beatrice's bedroom, and as expected, had ordered all the chambers thoroughly checked and the windows shut, but was too preoccupied with her attire to become hysterical over it. No doubt if the snake had been in *her* chamber it would have been a different matter.

Beatrice's anger at Gareth had lessened still further, and she was ready to be persuaded into forgiving him and his unjust accusations. She was ready, that is, until another incident made her furious at him once more.

Twenty Two

It was hard to decide who had provoked that unfortunate incident. Certainly Albinia's jealousy played a part in it, and it occurred after what seemed a very promising beginning to the evening.

After a sumptuous dinner, the squire gave his guests free choice. Those who wished to dance, to play cards, or to converse in the drawing room, were at liberty to pursue their preferences. An atmosphere of friendly informality permeated the party, and Sir Oliver, the captain, and the doctor rivaled the squire in amiability, and even the other guests seemed to thaw a little and looked at Lord Brook with less disapprobation and even some warmth. And judging from Camilla, one would never know she had been spurned by the baron. Her eyes glittered with venom only when she encountered Beatrice's eye, the look immediately veiled by lowered lids.

Camilla wore a satin gown of a fashionable yellow shade with a net overdress and large golden eardrops, but Beatrice thought riding dress suited her better.

The doctor and pastor and other gentlemen elected to play cards, some ladies chose to while away the time chatting, strolling along the terrace, while the squire himself led Albinia out for the first dance. Edgar stood up with Camilla, Sir Oliver and the captain with two other ladies. Beatrice was led onto the dance floor by her husband.

At first she hadn't been sure if he would ask her to dance, was not sure she wished him to. He stood by the door propping up the wall, glancing sardonically at Albinia and the squire, but the moment he noticed Edgar making for his wife, he stepped up to Beatrice and bowed. "May I have the honor of this dance?" he said stiffly, as if forcing the words out.

"To be sure," said Beatrice, feigning cool indifference. "We must at least preserve appearances."

He scowled. "There would have been no need for pretense if—" He broke off and bit his lip.

"If I hadn't poisoned you," she said sweetly, looking up into his face and smiling for the benefit of the onlookers.

"I wish I could believe otherwise," he said as he twirled her into the dance. She was unable to answer him for a moment, and when she could, she said, barely able to control the tremor in her voice, "If you had listened to my explanation, you would have believed me —or at least you should have." What a pity the sensuous strains of the waltz were wasted on them, she thought angrily.

But with the lovely music touching her senses and Gareth's strong arm twirling her about in the dance movements she loved, the magic of the waltz worked its charm and her countenance cleared. After all, perhaps when the squire had his talk with him, Gareth would apologize.

Lord Brook was thinking how lovely she looked. It was inconceivable to think she had made that attempt on his life. Had he been overhasty in jumping to conclusions? Perhaps he should have listened to her explanation. When the dance ended he would take her onto the terrace and give her the opportunity of persuading him of her innocence.

How well he dances, thought Beatrice. He was bending over her, his eyes locked on her face. Beatrice dared herself to look into them fully, and was lost. She read in them uncertainty, tenderness, and desire along with a mute plea for understanding. Her hurt and indignation at his conduct melted completely. Her breathing quickened as tenderness and love welled up within her. "Oh, Gareth," she whispered, "pray let us start anew." Had she said those words aloud? She must have, for a startled expression crossed his features for a moment, then dawning joy sprang to his eyes.

"Let us go onto the terrace," he said in a hoarse voice, and danced her toward the doors.

The strains of the waltz were still floating on the air and Gareth was twirling her about with joyful abandon. Beatrice shut her eyes and let her aroused feelings take over. To be held in his arms was a delicious ecstasy she had never experienced before. In this moment she knew with certainty that nothing mattered to her now except to be held close by Gareth, to spend a whole eternity in this blissful state.

And then they were alone on the terrace. His arms tightened about her. He should ask her for the explanation, he thought fleetingly. Instead he bent his head and his lips touched hers gently, tentatively at first. Then, as she did not shrink back or withdraw from him, but instead threw her arms around his neck, his lips searched hers with more insistence. They pressed onto hers in a ruthless, bruising kiss in which all his hurt, his hunger for love, and his desire of her found their full outlet at last. The music of the waltz had ceased, but they were not aware of it; nor of the graceful figure of Camilla standing in the doorway, a glass of punch in her hand, her face twisted with jealousy and rage.

Only when Camilla's cool contemptuous voice penetrated the cloud of bliss that surrounded them did they become aware of her presence, and sprang apart.

"I'll make allowances for a newlywed couple," Camilla, now standing beside them, said coldly, with strong censure, "but this is hardly the time or the place to behave this way." The words were most rude, and Beatrice, dismayed, hoped they were not overheard.

"A set is forming, and your host is seeking you to dance with him," Camilla said to Beatrice.

Lord Brook heaved a deep sigh. He was furious with Camilla and yet could not help but be grateful to her. She had brought him to his senses. He had almost forgotten himself. But the joy of Beatrice's kiss was still with him. She must be in love with him. She had to be. She had given her kiss to him wholly, without reservation or shrinking. But this indeed was not the time or the place for intimacy. Nor for exchanging confidences. Perhaps once they returned to Brook Manor . . .

Without answering Camilla's insult, he began to lead Beatrice back to the ballroom. Camilla followed at a leisurely pace. When they arrived at the doorway, the baron allowed his wife to precede him. Camilla reached the door at that precise moment also. She stumbled into Beatrice and her punch glass sloshed liquid onto Beatrice's lovely green gown.

Beatrice cried out in vexation, then she glanced at Camilla, fury in her eyes. "You did it on purpose," she cried.

Camilla shrugged. "You may think what you wish, Lady Brook," she said with a curling lip in a voice of chill hatred.

"Pray excuse me, Gareth, I must clean it off," said Beatrice in distress.

He started to say something, but the squire spied them and rushed forward. "Beatrice, what has . . . ?" His eyes glanced from the glass of punch in Camilla's hand to Beatrice's stained gown. "Come, I shall take you to the saloon. We shall clean this off in a trice," he said.

The orchestra was playing once more and the few couples were beginning to form a set.

"Are you not going to stand up with me, Gareth?" Camilla said mockingly, putting her punch glass on a side table.

"I'd rather stand up with a viper," he hissed in a low voice, but loud enough for Beatrice and the squire to hear. Beatrice felt great satisfaction, if not downright joy, at these words, and with a lighter heart she followed the squire across the ballroom floor.

They were leaving the room when suddenly Albinia pounced on them, her eyes glittering with suspicion. "Where are you taking her, Roger?"

"Camilla spilled some punch on her dress. I'm taking her to the saloon to clean it off."

"Well, she does not need *your* help to clean it up. Ring for a maid or . . ." She grabbed a passing footman and commanded, "Fetch some towels to the saloon. Lady Brook had an accident with her gown."

The squire, holding on to Beatrice's arm, said, "I'm taking her. She doesn't know where the saloon is."

"You have given us a tour. She should remember where it is. This is not Brook Manor. But if you wish, I shall take her."

The squire hesitated, but afraid that Albinia might make a scene, he consented.

"I trust this shan't spoil your enjoyment, Beatrice," he said, taking out his handkerchief and handing it to her to use on the gown.

"I don't think anything could spoil it now," she said, her eyes still full of stars.

Albinia, with one thing only on her mind, could interpret this remark in only one way. Her countenance twisted and her eyes glittered with jealousy. But she took Beatrice's arm and led her out and along the anteroom to the saloon—a handsome chamber decorated in blue and gold. She pointed to the sofa. "Sit down and a maid will be here directly. I am going back to the ballroom." She hesitated. "Remember, Beatrice, you are married to my brother. We Risboroughs do not tolerate divorce," she said as a parting shot, and marched out of the chamber, the color on her cheeks heightened, her bosom heaving in agitation.

Beatrice did not know whether to be vexed or amused. How could Albinia think she would throw over Gareth for the squire! The notion was preposterous. The squire was a very nice man, a good friend, but that was all. But that dreadful woman Camilla . . . Beatrice began to dab furiously at her gown with the handkerchief, and did not look up as footsteps sounded across the room. Thinking it was a maid, she said without lifting her head, "I hope you have dampened the towel. But I am afraid even that won't help." She broke off as she raised her head. It was not a maid who stood before her, but Edgar, his countenance full of concern.

"I know what occurred," he said, his voice sympathetic. "I saw her go onto the terrace. I am excessively sorry. But Camilla—" He bit his lip. "I have always been afraid her passion would provoke her into an incident like this. You must not mind her. She . . ." He took a big breath. "She seems to take her broken engagement to Brook as a good sport, but always bottling up her spleen and appearing unconcerned is not natural. Sometimes I am afraid that it will . . . Well, if she doesn't watch out, she might wind up in Bedlam," he suddenly said in a burst of confidence. "Here, pray let me dry it for you." He took the handkerchief from her and, kneeling, began to mop at the dress.

Beatrice was shocked. "You mean she might actually become queer in her attic? I thought Teswick was our only potential lunatic."

"Oh, Teswick is no lunatic," said Edgar, still intent on the gown. "She feels hostile toward you, for she loves Camilla. Naturally she would, Camilla is her niece, and she wished her to become the mis . . ." He broke off, startled, at what had slipped out.

"What? What did you say?" Beatrice asked incredulously, unconsciously placing a hand on his shoulder.

He looked up ruefully. "It slipped out. Pray keep it in confidence. I do hold Camilla in great esteem, but her jealousy is driving her to madness. And she cannot realize it is not your fault that you have supplanted her in Brook's home and affection."

"Yes, yes, but how . . . ?" She leaned forward eagerly. Such astonishing news.

Edgar rose from his knees and seated himself beside her. "I suppose I'd better tell you the whole, but it is a closely guarded secret, known only to our family, the Swintons, Teswick, and Camilla's abigail."

"But . . . but isn't Camilla's abigail the sister of Mrs. Teswick?"

He nodded. "To be sure."

"Then . . . then Camilla's abigail is . . ."

"Is her mother," supplied Edgar. "The child was born out of wedlock. Sir Oliver Swinton senior had a love affair with Camilla's mother, but he behaved in a very honorable way."

"He did not marry her," said Beatrice with asperity.

"My dear Beatrice, how *could* he? They were poles apart in social standing."

"Does Camilla know?"

"No. Oh, perhaps she suspects, but she doesn't know for sure, even though her mother would have preferred Camilla to grow up knowing the truth, grow up as her daughter, as the daughter of a domestic rather than a grand lady. It is difficult to comprehend such a wish."

"I can comprehend it," said Beatrice.

Edgar was dubious. "I don't know about that, but Teswick is the one who shows more maternal feeling for Camilla than her own mother. Teswick dotes on her. And she would do anything to please her."

Beatrice shook her head. What a complicated tangle. Her eyes fell back to her stained gown. "I'm afraid this won't come off," she said in a rather absentminded manner. Edgar began to rub the spot. Suddenly the handkerchief slipped from his fingers. He bent to retrieve it. So did Beatrice, automatically, her mind still on Camilla. Their heads bumped together.

Beatrice, startled, swayed, and Edgar steadied her by placing his hand on her shoulders. "I beg your pardon. I . . ." He was staring at her intently. "How beautiful you are," he whispered.

Beatrice grimaced with distaste. "Now, Edgar, you said you would behave with decorum."

"And so I shall, so I shall. But you present a temptation that is very hard to withstand."

His hand was still on her shoulder. He turned her gently toward him. "You have cast such a spell over me. Oh, Beatrice, Beatrice. I wouldn't hurt a hair on your head. And when I think . . ." His chest was heaving. The light of desire was in his eyes.

Beatrice became frightened. "Edgar, pray don't," she said, placing her hands upon his shoulders, meaning to push him back.

"Beatrice!" A shocked, hurt, and incredulous voice startled them, and Edgar jumped back, dismayed, and with every appearance of guilt.

Gareth stood on the threshold, his countenance twisted with fury and hurt, a damp towel dropping from his nerveless fingers. And beside him stood Camilla, a triumphant look on her face.

Twenty Three

With two strides Gareth was beside his bride. "So," he hissed at her, "I *was* right after all."

"Uncle, pray do not . . ." stammered Edgar. "I did not . . . This is not what you think."

Why does he behave like a dolt? thought Beatrice, irritated.

"Edgar, I need to speak to you immediately," said Camilla.

"Yes, yes, directly. Uncle, pray—"

"Go, go out of my sight before I forget myself, forget where we are and throttle you like the miserable, cowardly cur that you are." Lord Brook's wrath was frightening to see. His dark eyes were blazing with hatred and rage, his lips twisted in bitterness and pain.

"So, you are no different from all the rest," he said with a sneer, his rage and pain changing his features, making them almost unrecognizable.

Beatrice jumped to her feet, her own eyes blazing with outrage and indignation. "I am *not*. This is not what you think. I have never played you false."

"Oh, no," he said with deadly calm, stepping close to her and grabbing her shoulders in a painful grip. "I think you have," he said coldly, with deliberation. "I think you spoke the truth that day when you said you wished me dead. And you tried to bring this about."

"No! My God, no," cried Beatrice, wounded and dismayed by the dreadful paleness of his face, by the awful words he now apparently believed in.

"Oh, that horrible woman Camilla. It is all *her* fault," she cried in great exasperation.

He nodded gravely. "I agree that she is dreadful. But so are you." His lips pressed sharply into a thin line. "And I, fool that I was . . . My God, how you must have laughed at me, even when your lying lips deceived me with your kiss. The kiss of a Jezebel."

Beatrice stamped her foot. "I did not deceive you."

He took a menacing step forward. His arms shot up, his slender fingers closed around her throat. He was about to throttle her.

Beatrice became frightened. "Gareth, you are hurting me," she cried, turning pale.

Abruptly he flung her away from him. "I should wring your neck, but you are not worth my swinging on the gallows for," he said, his words dripping with loathing. "Do not be afraid"—another sneer twisted his features almost beyond recognition—"I shall never touch you again, Beatrice. I would rather touch a viper than you."

"And so would I. I would rather have gone to bed with that adder than you. And to think I wished you to make love to me." She laughed with derision and contempt. "You are a monster, Gareth Risborough, and I shall not remain under your roof a moment longer. I shall pack my things and leave you, and I don't care about propriety or keeping up appearances. You have your precious inheritance, that's why you married me. And I . . . I have saved my parents from debtors' prison. I shall pay back every penny of it to you, Gareth Risborough, if it takes me the rest of my life. But I shall never wish to see or speak to you again." And she turned around and fled in the opposite direction, not knowing where she was going, intent only on escaping from his awful presence.

Oh, how could she have been so blind as to deceive herself again and again to his true character? She hated him, hated him now with all the passion she had formerly felt at his kiss. She hated him and wished to see him humbled and hurt. But you *don't* wish to see him hurt, something screamed within her. She shut her ears to this scream. She wished *so* to see him hurt. She hated him.

Blinded by tears, she stumbled through chambers and corridors until she found herself on the terrace. The cold night air of the moor revived her somewhat. Shivering, she stared about her, uncomprehending at first; then she realized she stood on the terrace at the back of the house. The cold wind of the moor was blowing, chasing away the clouds in the night sky.

Beatrice wished she had her wrap with her. She walked slowly around the terrace to the side of the house. The light from the ballroom windows still streamed merrily into the shadows, but the musicians were packing up their instruments. And when she came to the corner of the terrace and looked over the front of the house, she observed that the squire was ushering his guests out. She hoped Camilla would be among them. The guests were going home. No doubt they had heard Gareth's and her shouted words. She did not care.

They were going home. She should do the same. Go home to her family, away from this monster that was her husband.

Slowly an idea was forming in her mind. She *would* go home. And the sooner the better. But first she must return to Brook Manor and pack her belongings. But how? She would not ride in the same carriage with him.

The path, the shortcut across the moor, stretched out before her like a silver ribbon. Dare she take it? With the full moon she could see well enough not to veer off. And if she but kept on going and the mist stayed away, in half an hour she should reach Brook Manor.

Burning with hatred of her husband, aching for swift action to assuage her hurt, she was already tripping down the terrace steps leading to the path. The sweet scent of the moors was a balm to her senses, if not to her soul. The wind acted bracingly on her body, but her mind was still in an agonizing turmoil as she stepped lightly onto the path. She should be safe here. Edgar would not dare to follow her, not at night. And the captain? He was not inebriated tonight. At least not yet. Besides, she had a head start on whoever might run after her.

With light, sure steps she began to run along the path across the moor.

Twenty Four

It was only after most of the guests had departed and the squire had a heart-to-heart talk with the baron that Beatrice's long absence was remarked upon and a search begun for her. Everybody knew Lady Brook had an accident with her dress, so her continued absence at first had not roused much concern. But when it finally dawned upon them that she was not on the premises, the different persons concerned reacted each in his or her own way, according to their character and feelings.

They searched for her, but she could not be found on the grounds of Cavanaugh Court. It was the squire who finally figured out that she must have taken the shortcut across the moor to Brook Manor. He immediately summoned Prince and made ready to start out after her.

Lord Brook wished to accompany him, but the guest who had been delayed by the storm, finally arrived and the baron was obliged to remain. The captain, who wished to search for Beatrice also, was astounded to see his sister and her child alight from the hired chaise, so naturally he decided to stay behind. Sir Oliver wanted to help the squire in his search, but the squire said the situation at Cavanaugh Court required the presence of someone with calm good sense to prevent emotions from getting out of hand. So the squire set out across the moor alone, save for Prince bounding by his side.

Albinia, diverted by the new arrivals, did not realize

at first that the squire had gone. When she did, she became furious and afraid. Furious at the thought of Roger and Beatrice alone on the moors, with only the stars and moon for company. And afraid because an accident might befall Roger. After all, he was not a young man and the moor was treacherous. She knew it well. She used to roam the moors in her childhood. What if he were to stumble and fall into a bog?

Never before had she contemplated that fact, nor faced her own emotions with honesty. Much as her fastidious nature resented it, she had to own to herself that she cared for the squire more than she realized. Had cared all these years, ever since—and she smiled at the memory—she had let his frog loose and he gave her the thrashing he thought she richly deserved.

Dear Roger. Her eyes became misty with tears and she scarcely saw the moor path gleaming in the moonlight.

That stupid old goat, she suddenly fumed, her mood changing mercurially. The old fool. Letting a fresh young face turn his head. She, Albinia, was not so old herself, and she was much more suitable for him than that shameless flirt Beatrice. Her brother's wife wouldn't get her claws into Roger. She, Albinia, *wouldn't* allow that to happen. She wouldn't let that harpy Beatrice make love to Roger on the moor.

At first she thought of enlisting someone to go with her, but discarded the notion at once. She did not wish any scandal. As it was, the story of Brook's and Beatrice's quarrel would be all over the countryside by tomorrow. Of course they had quarreled about Roger, and if Brook could be so whipped up with rage about it, it must be serious indeed. And then he was closeted with Roger for a time. Albinia could not hear what was being spoken, but she distinctly heard the name Beatrice. So what more proof did she need of the seriousness of the situation?

She would go after them at once. She hesitated. Her

slippers would be ruined. And her gown. Not to mention her constitution.

Her constitution . . .

For the first time in her selfish life she realized that without Roger her constitution did not matter to her very much. And her attire? She shrugged. She could always buy another ball gown. She determinedly started out across the moor.

She was at trifle apprehensive—the notion of falling into the bog was terrifying, but she had traversed this path as a child scores of times, and if only the fog kept away, she should have no problems.

Meanwhile, in the house Lord Brook was faced with a difficult decision. He wished to run after his wife at once, but he had to contain his impatience. He had been about to make some startling revelations, but his talk with the squire had convinced him that it would be wise to hold off a trifle longer. Thus he had to persuade the captain that his sister must remain a trifle longer "in the shadows," a very difficult task indeed.

Only when that was accomplished, and he had seen her settled with her child in one of the bedrooms, with the doctor in attendance—in case the child, still not quite recovered from the fever, needed help—could he turn his thoughts to Beatrice. He realized at almost the same time that his sister had disappeared.

From Camilla Lord Brook discovered that Albinia, convinced Beatrice meant to steal the squire from her, had run after him. He was surprised that she had dared to venture upon the moor. "She chose a fine time to own to herself that she is in love with Roger," he grumbled as he set out across the moor as well.

Twenty Five

Driven by an overwhelming sense of guilt and a fierce desire to humbly beg Beatrice's pardon and forgiveness, desperate that she would not heed him, and with good reason, the baron traversed the silent moor with great swiftness. It did not take him long to overtake Albinia.

He cut short her lamentations and her entreaties not to kill the squire. "Don't be more bird-witted than you are already," he told her roughly. "Turn back or wait here, just as you wish, but I must catch up with Beatrice. I have no time to spare for you now."

Albinia, watching her brother's grim countenance, quite pale in the moonlight, his lips tightly pressed and his eyes burning with a fierce determination, became convinced he meant to harm the squire. So while Gareth hastened on his way, she, wishing to prevent this calamity, trotted on after him.

Lord Brook, making quite good progress, soon far outdistanced her. The moon was now flitting in and out of the clouds, and mist began to rise on the moor. It was not very heavy yet, but it might obscure everything at any moment. He hoped with all his might that he would catch up with Beatrice before it did.

Beatrice shivered in the cold damp air. The wind on the moor had picked up, and wreaths of mist were rising from the bog. The moon kept playing hide-and-seek among the clouds, and at times the path across the moor was hardly visible.

At first Beatrice kept casting furtive glances behind her, but as she saw no one following her, she relaxed somewhat. Thus she was doubly startled and frightened when abruptly out of nowhere a dark shape materialized beside her. Her hair stood on end as legends of the black dog of Dartmoor leapt to her mind. But a friendly bark made her slump with relief and almost lose her footing.

"Prince! Good old Prince," she cried, overjoyed. She patted his head. "But where did you leave your master?" She squinted in the direction of Cavanaugh Court, but could not see much in the dark, with the mist creeping over the path.

"Did you come by yourself?" she asked. She would have welcomed the squire's presence, yet did not wish to call attention to herself by crying out to him. And she dared not take a chance on waiting for him—with the mist creeping over the moor—when she could not be sure if he were coming.

She hurried on, but kept glancing back from time to time. The last time she looked, she caught her breath. She was sure she saw a tall figure striding down the path. But it could not be the squire. The captain? She redoubled her pace and was glad of the dog's presence beside her.

With the mist muffling all sounds, she was not aware that somebody was upon her until Prince's barking alerted her. She whirled around. In the ghostly light of the moon she saw not the amiable face of the squire, but the pale grim countenance of her husband.

She gasped, turned around and fled, not seeing where she was going, veering off the path and right into the mire.

Prince began barking excitedly. "Beatrice, take care," cried Lord Brook, and sprinted after her. He caught her arm just in time. She tried to wrench free.

"Let me go. Let me go," she screamed.

"You little fool, what are you doing? You almost went into the mire," he shouted at her.

Startled, she stopped struggling and realized she was about to step into the morass. She gasped, gulped, then turned her head. "What if I did? Then you could have had your revenge. That should have made you very happy."

"Happy? Happy to see you dead? Oh, my God, Beatrice," he cried, wounded to the core. "I don't wish to see you dead. And I don't wish to see you hurt."

"No?" Beatrice was recovering her spirit. "You almost throttled me there in the saloon."

"I didn't know . . . I thought . . . I was consumed with jealousy. Beatrice, pray let me explain. Pray allow me to explain to you and beg your pardon."

But Beatrice's emotions got the better of her. "I don't wish to hear your explanations or apologies. I hate you, do you hear, Gareth Risborough, your lordship. I hate you. You have hurt me, you have insulted me, you thought me a murderess. You suspected me even today of making love to Edgar."

"No, no. I know I was wrong. Terribly wrong. And I have wronged you. I know now what must have occurred in the saloon and why. I know now about the snake. My God, if it weren't for Prince . . ." He shuddered and attempted to take her in his arms. She fought him off.

"That's a sudden change of mood, my lord," she cried, but her heart was pounding and her chest heaved.

"The squire told me the whole. I have been blind not to see it for myself, but he has opened my eyes. Beatrice, you must listen to me."

"Do you think I should wish to listen to you after all that you have said and done?" she cried scornfully.

"You must listen to me, or I shall go mad," he cried in a voice full of pain. "I love you, Beatrice."

"Now, that is a fine time to choose to tell me about it," she said sarcastically, but hot blood rushed to her cheeks.

He grabbed her arm, but she shook it free. "You are a trifle too late, my lord." But her voice sounded husky and she found it difficult to breathe. She could not stop a little thrill coursing through her body, even though she hated him. She caught herself. He had been too cruel to her, too unjust. Her wrath could not be so easily stilled. Besides, could she trust him again? At the slightest occasion he would accuse her again.

"Beatrice, I love you," he repeated in a hoarse voice, and attempted once more to take her in his arms.

"No. Pray let me go. I do not wish for your love anymore. You have killed any love I might have had for you. Pray let me go," she sobbed. "I never wish to see you again."

But he would not let her go. She began to struggle in earnest. "Let me go or we'll both tumble into the mud. Let me go." Both were oblivious of the barking and growling Prince.

They were forcibly reminded of him when suddenly, as Beatrice was tearing herself free and the baron was reaching after her again, the dog jumped between them, baring his teeth at Lord Brook as he once again came to Beatrice's defense.

"Prince, down," cried the baron, irritated., But the dog would not listen. He kept barking, quite loudly now, and growling menacingly.

"You misguided creature, *I* have a right to take her in my arms. I'm her husband," said Lord Brook, thoroughly exasperated.

"Good old Prince," cried Beatrice between laughter and tears. The baffled frustration on her husband's face was ludicrous to see. Prince kept jumping up on his legs, leaving mud prints all over his elegant breeches.

"Damnation. Down, Prince, down. Go home, you

idiotic hound. Beatrice, pray allow me to explain . . .''
He reached for her arm.

"He'll bite you," warned Beatrice.

"Damnation! I wish the squire hadn't let him loose,"
the baron cried.

"I wish the squire hadn't gone after your wife," an
indignant, plaintive voice interrupted their argument.

"Albinia, I cannot believe my senses," cried Beatrice.
It was hard to believe that this was the fastidious
Albinia. She seemed to be covered from top to bottom
in mud. Her hair was disheveled, and she had lost one of
her slippers. Never had Beatrice seen this elegant lady in
such a sorry state.

"Yes, it is I. No doubt you are surprised," Albinia
exclaimed. "But I shan't let you take Roger away from
me."

"Don't be an idiot, Albinia," the baron said sharply.

"And you—you monster, you knocked the poor man
down and he is even now unconscious, and you left him
there to die."

"What? The squire had an accident?" Beatrice exclaimed.

"An accident." Albinia snorted. "I should *say* he
had an accident. With my brother's fist."

"Did he say that?" barked the baron.

"He couldn't say anything. He had swooned before
he had a chance to do so."

"Gareth!" cried Beatrice.

"Don't you be an idiot, too," he snapped. "The
squire fell and hurt his ankle. That's all."

"Then why is he lying there unconscious, I should
like to know?" cried Albinia with indignation. The dog
was barking, excited by all the loud voices, and dancing
around them, not certain whom to attack, but ready to
defend Beatrice if need be.

The baron frowned. "He must have hurt his head
or . . ." His eyes narrowed in suspicion. Had Roger

done it on purpose, to shake some sense into Albinia? he wondered. "He seemed not to have been hurt much, and he begged me to go after you, Beatrice. He sent Prince after you too. He was concerned about your crossing the moor along at night."

"Oh, yes, he was concerned, the poor fool. But . . . Prince, stop that dreadful barking. Brook, make him stop."

The dog, hearing his name spoken in hostility, turned his attention to Albinia, jumping up her skirt.

"Shoo, go away," Albinia screamed. "You'll dirty my gown with your paws."

"But . . . but, Albinia," said Beatrice, suppressing her desire to giggle, "you're already c-covered with mud."

Albinia's face fell. She glanced at her muddied gown with resignation and despair.

"What happened to you? You look as if you've had a mud bath," said Beatrice.

"I fell. I was running too hard, and these slippers are not made for moor walking." She glanced at her one remaining muddied slipper with distaste, lifted her leg and jerked the slipper off, and threw it in the bog. "You're of no use to me. Go join your mate. Well, are you two going to just stand there gaping? Go and help the squire. Do something. Fetch help."

"Albinia, you *do* care about Roger!" exclaimed Beatrice.

"Of course I care," said Albinia, her chest heaving. "I always did. But if I'd married him, he would have dragged me all over the moor. I couldn't stand that. But rather than have him entrapped by you or some other designing female, I'd even make *that* sacrifice." She turned to her brother. "Go help him, you brute."

The dog was still barking. "Prince, stop that infernal racket," shouted the baron. "Beatrice, I must have speech with you. I cannot just let you walk out of my

life. Pray listen to me, I do humbly beg your pardon.''
He took Beatrice's arm.

Beatrice stepped back. "Take care,'' she cried, and
Prince jumped in front of her again.

"You can beg her pardon as much as you like, but
later,'' Albinia reproved him. "Now, go and help
Roger. Ohh,'' she suddenly moaned, clutching at her
heart. "Ohh, I'm having such palpitations. Ohh, I'm
going to have a spasm.''

"She has recalled her 'delicate constitution,' '' said
Lord Brook with a grimace.

"Well, today she can be believed, with reason,'' said
Beatrice.

"Beatrice, I cannot allow you to slip away from me.''
He tried to pull her to him. The dog threw himself at
him, and only with luck the baron escaped his sharp
teeth.

"I shall swoon at once,'' moaned Albinia. "Ohh, will
nobody help me. And poor Roger. Ohh.'' She swayed
and tottered on her feet.

"Talk about Cheltenham tragedies,'' said the baron,
gritting his teeth.

Beatrice did not know whether to be angry or
amused. Her feelings for her husband had tumbled and
skyrocketed so much in this last short space of time, she
felt dizzy. She realized she needed solitude and calm
reasoning to sort them out. He had hurt her dreadfully,
and she hated him. She never wished to see him again,
and yet perversely she also wished to hear him say again
that he loved her. She took a deep breath.

"You must go and succor the squire,'' she said in a
much more composed tone, "while I go with Albinia to
Brook Manor. Prince can go with us.''

"No need to succor the squire. He has succored himself.''

"Roger,'' screamed Albinia. "Thank God, you are
not dead.'' And she threw herself into his arms. He

promptly folded them around her, but said sharply, "Take care, my ankle. There, there . . ." he patted her. "I'm still alive and intend to remain so for some time to come." But he was unable to support her to Brook Manor. Beatrice lent her an arm, while the baron helped the squire to hobble forward. Thus, with Prince leading the way, they traversed the last lap of the path, wading through soggy heather, Albinia moaning about her poor feet as they made their way to Brook Manor.

In the general confusion that ensued after they entered the hall, Beatrice slipped away to her chamber and locked herself in. She could not face Gareth tonight. She must be much clearer in her mind how she felt about him before deciding whether to forgive him, whether to listen to his apologies at all. Reluctantly she took a dose of laudanum, as she needed rest, and after such tumultuous experiences it would have been impossible for her to fall asleep. She drifted off with Lord Brook's words, "I love you" repeating themselves in her mind.

Beatrice awoke when the sun was high on the horizon. From her maid she discovered that Lord Brook had made several attempts to see her, but had finally given up. And now he had departed, taking the squire back to Cavanaugh Court. Beatrice felt dissatisfaction at this last intelligence, although that had been the right thing to do. And after all, she had been asleep.

The next information, however, made her sit bolt upright in bed with anger. Camilla and Sir Oliver had come to the manor. Camilla had attempted to speak with Lord Brook privately. Whether she had done so, the maid was not sure, but if was shortly afterward that he departed for Cavanaugh Court. Camilla and Sir Oliver were still in the house, chatting with Edgar.

Beatrice did not wish to meet them, especially not Camilla. She had breakfast—prepared by her own maid —sent up, dressed hastily, and slipped out the side door of the manor to go for a walk on the moor. Mindful of the unwritten rules, she had told her maid she would go up to the nearest tor and in the solitude of the moor seek solace and advice. She would have liked to take Prince along with her, but though the squire had left him on guard at the door to her bedchamber, he was not there now. Most likely the squire had taken him back with him when he left this morning. Looking for the dog, or even sending her maid to look for him, might call attention to herself.

Beatrice had believed herself unobserved when she left the manor, but a maid chancing to look out the window saw her make for the moor. And gossiped about it in the kitchen. In no time at all this information reached Teswick's, then Camilla's ears. A short time later Camilla, her eyes burning with hatred, frustration, and rage, strode out of the manor in Beatrice's wake. Keeping well behind and seeking cover in some bushes, she stalked Beatrice as she would stalk a wild animal she intended to hunt down.

Meanwhile Beatrice strode on, letting the fresh breeze caress her brow and cool her body and mind. Should she forgive Gareth? She could not be sure. Her thoughts were still confused. Did she love him? An ache in her heart answered her, but after his cruel words, how could she be sure it would be lasting? Could she ever forget the hurt he had inflicted upon her, even were she to forgive it? She resolved not to make any decisions at once, but let her mind wander freely and relax. The right decision would come to her by and by.

She became calmer the farther she went, until she came to the massive rocks of the tor. She recalled when Brook had taken her to the top. And on an impulse she began to climb. When she finally stood at the summit, with the whole panorama of the moors stretched out before her, she felt peace settle in her heart at last.

Brook deserved a second chance, she abruptly decided. What more hurt could she risk, by giving him that chance, than she had experienced already? He said he loved her. If that could but be true . . . A sudden exultation possessed her. She would give herself only to the man she loved, after all, as she had vowed to do.

She stared at the splendid panorama, but in her mind's eye she saw stretching before her the years ahead in the company of Gareth, the man who loved her and whom she loved in return.

Sunk in such blissful reverie, she was quite unaware of the stealthy approach of Camilla as she scrambled silently upon the tor, creeping ever closer and closer, the glitter of hatred in her eyes.

Twenty Six

In Squire Cavanaugh's drawing room Lord Brook was taking leave of the squire. The baron was eager to return to the manor, although, believing his wife would get up quite late, he was sure he would be back before she awakened.

He had been on the point of departure for Cavanaugh Court when Sir Oliver and Camilla arrived at the manor. The squire advised Lord Brook to remain, but the baron, who had promised to talk to the captain in the morning, worried that he might not keep his mouth shut about his sister if he did not keep his promise.

With Sir Oliver present, neither Camilla nor Edgar could get up to any tricks. And with Beatrice in her chamber and Prince guarding the door, she should be safe until he returned, which would be soon. So he reasoned.

He was to be proved wrong in his reasoning when the footman admitted a breathless, frightened maid, liberally splashed with mud, who had come from Brook Manor and desired to speak to his lordship.

She bobbed a shaky curtsy and glanced uneasily at the squire.

"You can speak freely in front of the squire. He is my friend," said Lord Brook. Then, struck by a foreboding that made his heart grow cold, he added, "Has something untoward happened to Lady Brook?"

The maid nodded vigorously. "Leastways, it might have. Mrs. Teswick said so. She said to give your lordship this message: Lady Brook is in great danger, and you are to hasten back. She will tell you the whole. Oh pray, sir, do make haste. And pray tell me, your lordship, if there's anything *I* can do to help."

"Is Lady Brook still in her chamber?"

"No, sir. That I do know. For I was fetching her the gown I had mended for her, and she wasn't there."

"Oh, my God, the little fool," cried the baron, becoming paler still. "Where is Lady Brook now?" he asked sharply, cold fear coiling around his heart.

"That I do not know. I fancy Mrs. Teswick does."

"Right. Much obliged. You may go."

The servant turned to go. The squire put up a hand. "One moment. I left Prince guarding Lady Brook."

"Your dog, sir?"

"Yes."

"I collect Miss Risborough's maid, knowing how her mistress hates dogs, ordered him taken away."

"I shall wring Albinia's neck," said the squire with feeling.

The baron strode to the door. "I'm off, Roger."

"Across the moor?"

The baron hesitated. "Perhaps I shouldn't. If I borrow one of your horses and take the road at a gallop, I might be there about the same time. I can't afford to twist *my* ankle at this time. And I doubt I could force myself to walk with caution."

The squire nodded. "Very wise. I'll ride with you."

A moment later the two friends were galloping away down the road, while Jean, having caught her breath, started back across the moor.

The two men made it to Brook Manor in reasonably good time. The baron jumped from his horse and ran to the kitchen, where Mrs. Teswick, having dismissed all the servants, was standing wringing her hands, wiping tears away with her apron, her cold composure having deserted her for once.

The squire, having swung himself somewhat stiffly off his mount, followed the baron.

"Where is my wife? Who wishes to kill her?" snapped Lord Brook at the housekeeper, his countenance hard as flint, his voice icy cold. Under his outward calm, terror gripped his heart.

"Ah, no, no. I cannot believe it . . . and I cannot be sure," moaned Mrs. Teswick. "Your lordship's telling her you loved Lady Brook and would always love her—that did something to her. She . . . she became . . . She . . . she seemed to lose her reason after that. She always hoped, at least I fancied she did . . ."

The baron released a long breath.

So Camilla was the one.

"Where are Miss Swinton and my wife?"

"Her ladyship went for a walk on the moor, and Ca . . . Miss Swinton went after her."

"Which direction precisely?" he rapped at her.

"I do not know. But her ladyship's maid would know."

"Fetch her."

At this moment Pedmore, hearing agitated voices in the kitchen, poked his head in the doorway.

"Fetch Lady Brook's abigail at once," the baron commanded him.

"Very good, sir," Pedmore said, and withdrew.

"It was Camilla who drugged Beatrice, and with your contriving," the baron grimly accused the housekeeper. "And drugged me. And put the snake in my wife's bed." As he turned toward the door, he encountered the squire, a stern expression on his amiable countenance.

"Ah, no, no," moaned Mrs. Teswick, "the Wistman's Wood thing—yes. I put the laudanum in Lady Brook's preserves. I did it for *her*. It seemed a

harmless prank," she wept. "We were sure her ladyship
would not attempt to cross the moor at night, so no real
harm would come to her. It was wrong, I know, but not
meant to kill."

The baron was by the door. The housekeeper rushed
after him. "I did not know about the snake. *That* could
have killed her ladyship." Despair rang through her
sobs. "I did not know. She did it by herself. She just
told me to keep her ladyship's maid occupied in the
kitchen. She did not tell me why. Oh, pray, believe me."
Suddenly she became conscious of the squire, gulped,
and squared her shoulders. "And I never drugged your
lordship. Nor did she. After the snake, I watched. I
watched her that day. She couldn't have done it."

"It could have been Edgar, borrowing Camilla's
method," the squire said, in a low tone. "I suspect
Edgar has his finger in this pie somewhere."

"Oh, no doubt of it," the baron said, and to Mrs.
Teswick: "I shall deal with you later," his tone boding
her no good. "Now, go and tell them to saddle Fencer at
once."

The woman took a deep breath, straightened her
shoulders even more, and marched out quickly through
the opposite door to the servants' quarters.

The baron bit his lip. "I'm sorry if I have been the
cause of her losing her reason, but I could not have done
otherwise. I could not have married her."

"No need to tell *me* that, old boy. I wish I could go
with you. Take Prince. He'll help."

The baron scowled. "Not me, he won't. Well, I shall
take him anyway." He pressed the other's hand
fleetingly. "Thanks, Roger, for everything." And he
rushed out of the house. A few moments later he was
galloping Fencer toward the moor.

Twenty Seven

Beatrice became aware of Camilla's presence when she suddenly heard heavy breathing behind her, and, startled, whirled around. Her eyes widening in fright and dismay, she gasped out, "Camilla, how did you know where to find me?" For of course Camilla had come here after her on purpose. Beatrice's heart began to pound in increased apprehension.

"Oh, I have friends at the manor," Camilla said, her face distorted with jealousy and rage.

"You mean Teswick?" asked Beatrice numbly.

Camilla nodded.

"But I did not tell the housekeeper where I was going. I told nobody but my maid. And she would not gossip about it."

"You did not seriously think you could sneak out of the house with nobody seeing you do so?" Camilla asked scornfully.

"Yes, I did," said Beatrice, nettled. "I made sure there was nobody about in the yard."

"You forgot the windows. Somebody chanced to see you go. You are a prime topic for gossip in the servants' quarters."

"Why are you here?" But she knew why. Cold fear clutched at her heart as she read the murderous intent in Camilla's eyes.

"No, no," she whispered. Then, rallying, in a louder

voice: "You wished to kill me all along. You drugged me and put the snake in my bed. And you drugged Gareth."

"No!" The denial came sharp and swift. "That was Edgar's own foolish notion. I never would have allowed it."

Edgar too—both of them. Suddenly Beatrice's knees turned to blancmange. The pleasant moor breeze now felt icy cold, and she could hardly prevent her teeth from chattering. She would be missed, she thought desperately. Oliver and Edgar . . . But Edgar was Camilla's accomplice. "Surely your brother could not have known about it," she cried.

"Of course not," agreed Camilla with scorn.

"I comprehend your reason for hating me, but why would Edgar wish to harm Gareth?"

Camilla glanced at her with contempt. "You are dull-witted today. For the inheritance, of course."

"What?"

"Well, of course. You must have known that he would inherit both the title *and* the estate. As long as Gareth was not married, Edgar could afford to wait for his uncle to break his neck while riding or driving. He felt it was only a question of time. Even if Gareth had married Evelyn, things would not have become desperate. We felt sure their marriage would not have been consummated. With you"—her lip twisted in distaste and hate—"with you it was different. Edgar could not afford to have his uncle sire a child. *That* had to be prevented at all costs. At first we did our best to keep you and Brook at odds with each other, to give you a distaste for life on the moor. But"—and there was a grudging look of respect in her eyes—"you proved tougher than we anticipated. Even the specter and the eerie laugh did not scare you off. So I told Edgar to do something. But instead of getting rid of *you*, he attempted to kill Gareth in this clumsy, unsatisfactory way. And he had the temerity to take *me* to task for putting the snake in your bed. The fool was actually developing a *tendre* for you.''

Camilla ground her teeth. ''But I would have none of it. You have stolen Gareth away from me, but you shall not take Edgar. In fact, I have decided to make sure you shan't stand in my way any longer.''

Beatrice's throat was dry. ''How will that help you? I don't think Gareth will wish to marry you. After all, he had cried off from your engagement.'' That was the wrong thing to say, she realized at once, as Camilla took one step forward, her face becoming even more distorted with hate.

''If he does not, I shall have my revenge,'' she said viciously.

Beatrice licked her dry lips and swallowed hard. Fighting down the panic that threatened to engulf her, she tried to reason with Camilla. ''I don't think you should do anything hasty. After all, people will know you have come after me.''

''Nobody knows but Teswick, and *she* will keep her mouth shut.''

Despair twisted itself around Beatrice's heart like a cold vise.

Camilla was inching closer. Her intent was quite clear —to push Beatrice off the tor, so she would be dashed to pieces on the ground below. Nobody could prove she had not fallen accidentally.

''So now, my lady,'' said Camilla, ''this is where you cease to be a hindrance to me.'' Her arms rose.

Beatrice caught her breath, and glancing desperately around, darted to the side, almost slipping on the moss-covered rock, and tried to scramble down.

But Camilla was too quick for her. ''Oh no, you shan't escape me,'' she hissed.

Beatrice felt this was a waking nightmare as Camilla grabbed her and began to push her to the edge of the rock.

"No, no," Beatrice screamed, struggling to remain where she was. But Camilla seemed to be possessed of superhuman strength. Inexorably she kept pushing and pulling Beatrice ever closer to the edge.

Beatrice screamed again. Too intent on survival, she was not aware of her surroundings, not aware of anything save the death-dealing presence of Camilla. Panting, heart hammering, she kept kicking out and attempting to wrench herself from Camilla's grip. She could not. She slipped and fell, but locked in deadly combat with Camilla, she pulled her down with her. The two rolled over and over, hurting and bruising their bodies, but Camilla did not seem to feel any pain. They were struggling quite close to the edge now, Camilla still trying to push Beatrice off the tor.

Beatrice would not let go of her, yet Camilla, panting, eyes glittering with an insane hatred, was gaining the upper hand. Her hands abruptly fastened on Beatrice's throat and squeezed.

Beatrice tried to scream, but her breath was cut off. The veins on her temples bulged. Her eyes started from their sockets and her lungs were aching for air. Panic-stricken, she struggled on, trying to pry open those steely fingers.

Camilla, disregarding Beatrice's kicks and clawing fingers, her hands clamped around Beatrice's throat, was shoving her over the edge. Beatrice's head and shoulders were hanging over the precipice, but so were Camilla's as she tried to squeeze the life out of Beatrice's body.

Beatrice felt her senses grow dim. She was losing consciousness.

And Camilla's countenance broke into a hideous grin of malicious triumph.

Twenty Eight

As if from a great distance, Beatrice heard the barking of a dog, and abruptly the pressure on her throat was eased and she was choking and gasping for air. Her eyes flew open.

Prince, barking and baring his teeth at Camilla, stood over them.

"Go away, Prince," Camilla shouted. But the dog only jumped closer and continued his excited barking.

"Prince," croaked Beatrice. "Prince, help."

"Prince, stay out of it. Go home, go back to the squire."

The dog barked at her. He did not throw himself at her, but his stance was certainly menacing. He growled.

"I see that you won't listen to me. Well, I hate to do it to you, but you *are* a nuisance." A knife materialized in her hand.

"No," Beatrice screamed, her own danger momentarily forgotten. "Don't kill Prince."

"She is not going to kill anyone," a hard, cold voice suddenly announced above them, and Lord Brook, very pale, lips tightly pressed and terrible rage in his eyes, was standing beside them. In his hand he had a pistol, pointed at Camilla.

"It you make one move, Camilla, I shall shoot you," he said with deadly calm.

But Camilla only shook her head. "No, you won't.

You're too much of a gentleman for that. You can cry off from an engagement to a lady, but not kill her."

"Camilla, I mean it."

But Camilla was beyond reasoning. Disregarding the cocked pistol and the dog, she suddenly gave Beatrice a mighty shove. Beatrice screamed as her body, hanging precariously above the precipice, overbalanced. It seemed she was falling, but she had enough presence of mind to grab at Camilla's arm. Prince barked in agitation, and Lord Brook, forgetting the pistol, dropped to his knees to grab Beatrice.

Camilla tried both to push Beatrice off the cliff and to free her own arm as Beatrice and Lord Brook endeavored to prevent her from sending Beatrice to her death.

For a moment all was confusion, a tangled mass of arms and legs as the three of them struggled at the very edge of the tor.

Then Beatrice, with Lord Brook's help, managed to pry Camilla's hands loose, and suddenly Camilla, with a scream of terror, toppled over and fell.

Beatrice would have been swept along, but for Lord Brook's strong arms, which were almost wrenched out of their sockets, holding on to her as she hung over the precipice. Slowly he pulled her to safety.

Drenched with perspiration, Beatrice fell into his arms. "Oh, Gareth, Gareth," she sobbed with hysterical relief.

He enfolded her in a strong embrace, stroking her head and murmuring soothing words. "It is over now, my darling, my love. You are safe. And I love you." Then he cupped her face in his hand and began gently to kiss away her tears.

The dog, who had been barking and jumping about, not knowing whom to attack, now stopped his frenzy. He cocked his head and regarded the couple quizzically. Then he gave a happy bark and began to wag his tail.

* * *

Camilla had not been killed by her fall. She had not
fallen to the ground below, but to a closer ledge, and she
was alive when the grooms from the manor came to
rescue her. She had a broken arm and had some other
injuries—how grave, it was not yet known. She was unconscious when she was taken to the manor. Sir Oliver
was saddened, shocked, and concerned about the
whole. He begged Beatrice's pardon and explained that
he had suspected that Camilla's unnatural resignation to
her fate hid a volcano of restrained emotions that had
finally broken through.

Beatrice, feeling quite sympathetic toward him,
accepted his apology—after all, he was not to blame for
his sister's actions—and said, "You probably blame my
husband for the whole."

But to her surprise, Sir Oliver shook his head. "You
mean because he cried off?" He shook his head. "Don't
blame Brook. Must have had good reason. Know my
sister, you see." Which was quite magnanimous of him
in the circumstances.

He said he would send Camilla to some relations in
Ireland, if she survived. Neither Lord Brook nor
Beatrice wished to see her arrested or put in Bedlam,
and Oliver would make sure she would be well cared for
and well guarded as well.

Throughout the course of all this, Edgar kept up a
pious pretense of being shocked, commiserating with
Beatrice and his uncle and Sir Oliver and generally
conducting himself in a way which made Beatrice, who
now knew the truth about him, quite nauseated.
Obviously he was not aware she knew the truth, and
Gareth still seemed to think Camilla was responsible for
drugging him. Or perhaps he just did not wish to talk
about it in the presence of others. Beatrice longed to be
along with him, to warn him that while they had
disposed of one murderer, the other still remained.

Finally Sir Oliver left and Camilla was taken away.

Albinia was reclining in the back parlor with a wet cloth on her brow. In spite of being prepared by the squire, she was prostrated by the shocking event. Lord Brook and the squire were discussing something in the hall. Only Edgar and Beatrice remained in the drawing room.

Edgar came over to stand over Beatrice as she reclined on the pink damask sofa. "What a dreaful ordeal for you, Beatrice," he said. "Indeed, you are the most remarkable female of my acquaintance. Nothing that ever happens to you has the power to daunt you. You have my greatest admiration."

Beatrice's self-control deserted her. "But that admiration did not restrain you from something you knew must bring me great pain," she cried angrily. "It did not stop you from trying to kill my husband. Your own uncle," she added bitterly.

Edgar, becoming pale, stood still, speechless for a moment. Then he rallied. "I cannot comprehend it, Beatrice. You wound me deeply by—"

"Oh, don't be so hypocritical, and don't lie," snapped Beatrice. "Camilla told me the whole, there on the tor. She was responsible for drugging me and for the snake. And I daresay, now that I think of it, for provoking me to ride on Fencer and go walking alone in Wistman's Wood, but you—you tried to kill Gareth."

Edgar licked his dry lips. "My dear Beataice," he began in distress, "how can you believe the babble of a demented woman? That just proves that she is a Bedlamite."

"She may be that," a broken voice said behind them, "but she did not poison his lordship. I can swear to that. And I can also swear that you did it."

Mrs. Teswick, eyes reddened and swollen from tears, trembling and hardly able to keep on her feet, entered the room and stood stiff and straight before them. "The hamper was in the hall on the table, with the bottle of wine. I knew you would put the blame on her for that too. So I questioned the servants. One footman happened to see you standing beside the hamper uncorking the wine bottle. It was just a glimpse, but he can swear to it."

"Lies, all lies," Edgar croaked.

"He can swear to it in a court of law, and I can swear that she could not have done it," the housekeeper said triumphantly. "I shan't let you lay this at her feet, the poor lamb."

Poor lamb? Poor tiger or poor snake, Beatrice thought with a curling lip.

"And let me tell you, Master Edgar, that if it hadn't been for you, with your fine airs and manners and your taking ways with females, she wouldn't be in this sorry state now. If she lives at all." She strangled a sob. Her hands were shaking.

Beatrice took a deep breath. "Thank you, Mrs. Teswick. You have been most helpful. I shall speak to you anon. Now, pray leave us."

And as the housekeeper turned and marched out on trembling legs, only at the very door letting her body sag, Edgar took out his handkerchief and wiped his perspiring forehead. "Phew, you don't really believe her, do you, Beatrice?" he asked in a somewhat hoarse but cajoling voice.

"But we believe her, m'boy." The squire's voice was almost jovial, but his countenance was grim. Lord Brook, his face a hard mask, his lips tightly pressed, stared at his nephew accusingly.

"It would be much better for you if you owned to your dastardly deed," said the squire. "For we know how to make you confess. We, both of us, shall take you to the Cranmere—at night—and shall leave you there . . . alone. I'm sure that by morning you'll be a babbling imbecile ready to admit everything."

It was cruel, but it might be effective, thought Beatrice, observing the sudden look of terror on Edgar's face.

"And don't think we can't do it, for we can. And nobody will lift a finger to help you. You may be liked by the domestics, but they definitely don't hold with killing the master of the house."

"You . . . you all belong in Bedlam," Edgar said in a quavering voice, his eyes wide with fear.

"Edgar, if you confess now, you shan't end up in Newgate," Beatrice said. "Will he, my lord?"

Lord Brook's eyes softened for a moment as he glanced at her. Then his expression hardened. "I don't wish for any more scandal—if it can be avoided. But his confession I must have. At all events, whether you confess now or not, you might as well know that you shan't be living at Brook Manor anymore. And no longer can you count on me to give you money. Under the circumstances, Newgate would be the only accommodation you could afford."

Edgar bit his dry lips. He seemed to have shrunk, wilted. He did not even look handsome anymore. "And if I confess?"

"Sign a written confession and I shall settle a generous sum on you—provided you don't show your face in England again. Go to Ireland, near Camilla, where you can console each other."

"A splendid notion," said the squire. "For *you*. Though for my part I would prefer to see you on the gallows."

Abruptly Beatrice was struck by a thought. "Edgar, how could you bring yourself to attempt killing your own uncle? Whatever else you may have done, I would never have supposed you to be capable of that."

"To be quite honest with you, I thought he would be too cowardly to do it," said Lord Brook.

"Even a rat can fight, if cornered," supplied the squire. "And Edgar certainly fits that description."

"No, not a rat, more a mouse," said Lord Brook with scorn.

Edgar's cheeks were burning with mortification.

"You have one redeeming feature, Edgar. You truly did not wish *me* harmed," said Beatrice, making herself sound sympathetic.

Lord Brook scowled.

Edgar, thankful to hear a kinder voice, grabbed at her words. "Ah, you know, Beatrice, that I didn't."

"Yet you were willing to cause me great distress by killing my husband."

"I fancied I could make you forget him."

Lord Brook's countenance became a thundercloud, and he took a step forward. The squire placed a restraining hand on his arm and put a finger to his own lips, shaking his head.

Lord Brook subsided.

"And," Edgar suddenly blurted out, "I would not have attempted it, had Camilla not kept nagging at me to do something to prevent the consummation of your marriage. Well, *I* did not want that either. So what else could I do? I tried everything, and still I could not keep you two apart."

Beatrice's eyes, shining like stars, looked at her husband, and he threw her a soft loving glance.

"Will you sign a confession, Edgar?" rapped out the squire.

"Sign? Oh, I . . ." He passed his hand distractedly across his face. "I have confessed already, haven't I?" He shrugged and wet his dry lips. "So . . . I lose. But if you had drowned there in the bog—"

"You wouldn't have succeeded Brook in any case," said the squire. "There is a young child who would have inherited all."

"How have one rethinking leading, forgive You truly had act out a have hold of." said Beatrice, masking herself

Twenty Nine

Edgar was quite stunned. "A child? You mean a bastard of my uncle's?"

"Could that be true?" Beatrice could not help feeling dismayed, even though Captain Tremblay had intimated his sister's child was sired by Lord Brook.

The baron opened his mouth, but the squire silenced him. "The less he knows now, the better. Later he shall discover it, but by then he'll be out of England."

"Go and pack your things," Lord Brook ordered. "I want you to be out of here today."

Edgar glanced helplessly and with deep regret around the room. "Leave all this, my home," he said in a low hopeless voice.

"Edgar," Beatrice said, feeling sorry for him in spite of all, "it is much better to be away from home but alive and reasonably well provided for than to languish in Newgate or swing on the gallows."

Edgar's face brightened perceptibly. "You are right, of course. And who knows . . ." A speculative look crept into his eyes.

"Ireland is full of comely colleens, and some of them are quite plump in the pocket," said the squire. "Now, just pack and then come here to sign a confession. You will be out of here before the magistrate comes."

"The magistrate?" Edgar sprang to his feet, alarmed. "What for?"

"To take the statement from us about Camilla,

naturally. The servants are better than a town crier for spreading the news.''

Edgar was shocked into quick action. ''I am on my way. Beatrice,'' he sighed, ''I deeply regret to have been obliged to hurt you. I wish things could have been otherwise.'' He glanced with dislike at his uncle. For the first time Beatrice saw that look. ''It will be a relief not to pretend liking for you, Uncle,'' he said. ''Good-bye, Beatrice.'' And he dashed out of the room.

A short silence followed. Then, it seemed as if upon a signal from the squire, the baron crossed the floor after his nephew. ''I shall write out a confession for him to sign,'' he said. ''I shall be back directly.''

The squire and Beatrice were left alone. The squire went over and sat down beside her and patted her hand. ''Well, child, all is well that ends well. Is that not so?''

Beatrice frowned. ''Yes, of course. But about his child . . .''

''Let Brook tell you about that. I have something else of a delicate nature to impart to you. Something that Brook himself could never bring himself to say to you,'' he said gently.

''What is that?''

''Simply this. I'm sure you wish to know the reason for Brook's breaking his engagement to Camilla.''

''Oh, yes,'' cried Beatrice eagerly. ''I wished to ask him that, but I dared not.''

''I'm glad you didn't. It is a very painful subject to him. The reason is simple, and not, unfortunately, terribly unusual, and accounts for my strong dislike of Edgar.''

''Edgar?''

He nodded. ''Brook came from the wars a hero—a wounded, very ill hero. I have told you that. His convalescence was long and slow. For a time, even his doctors despaired of his ever walking again. But he contrived to fool them all.

"Brook excelled in sports. But that you know also. Camilla, as well, enjoyed sports, and to give the devil her due, was always a fearless and daring creature.

"Brook came home, a man seemingly physically broken. Camilla"—the squire's lips curled with distaste —"Camilla did not show any of the finer feelings for him, certainly not love. Instead"—the squire's voice shook a little—"she held him in disgust because of his infirmities."

"Oh, the beast," cried Beatrice with indignation.

"Precisely. So I thought. To resume, while Brook was away earning his hero's orders, Camilla consoled herself with Edgar. He was quite taken with her and—"

"They had been lovers?" Beatrice asked quickly.

The squire shrugged. "I do not know. But I do know —and believe me, it was with the greatest difficulty that Brook revealed the whole to me—that, coming home unexpectedly, he caught them kissing and embracing. Not only that, he heard Camilla make disparaging remarks about his lameness, his lack of strength. His condition gave her a disgust of him, she said.

"After this, Brook demanded Camilla to cry off. He could no longer contemplate marriage with her. But Camilla would not. She never dreamed that Brook would do the unbelievable—cry off himself."

Beatrice released a long breath. "That dreadful witch," she cried. "Oh, poor Gareth. How he must have suffered."

"So now that you know the whole, you can understand better his reaction and his jealousy of Edgar. He thought the same thing was happening again between you and Edgar."

"Yes, but I am *not* the same as Camilla," Beatrice said, much outraged.

"Quite true. I realized that at the very outset. But Brook has been shockingly unknowing where women are concerned. But now that that situation is corrected, I must return to Cavanaugh Court. I have been away far too long. I'll just take leave of Albinia.''

Beatrice thanked the squire warmly. She would have thanked Prince also, but he had been banished from the house on Albinia's orders. Beatrice thought that Albinia might as well get used to having Prince around if she intended to marry the squire, which the squire, with a roguish twinkle in his eye, told her Albinia had at last agreed to do.

As Beatrice accompanied the squire to the hall, she abruptly heard a loud bark coming from the back of the house and Albinia's plaintive voice, ''What *are* you doing here? Who let you out?''

Squire Cavanaugh made a comical grimace. ''Oh-oh. He must have escaped from the kennels.'' He limped hurriedly toward the corridor that ran behind the great hall and off which opened the private dining room and back parlor.

''Shoo, go away,'' Albinia's irritated voice sounded again. Followed by a friendly unrepentant bark.

''I don't want her overset any more than she is already,'' the squire said worriedly as he and Beatrice rounded the corner.

Beatrice's eyes opened wide and the squire's countenance broke into a wide grin. Prince was standing beside Albinia, wagging his tail, and Albinia—her vinaigrette still clutched in one hand—was hesitantly patting his tawny head. She looked up on hearing their footsteps and snatched the hand away.

''I'm going back to Cavanaugh Court,'' said the squire, while the dog bounded toward him and Beatrice. Beatrice bent and hugged the intelligent animal, whose tail wagged furiously. ''Thank you for saving me,'' she whispered.

Then she straightened, ''I'll take Prince outside, Roger, while you say your good-byes to Albinia,'' she offered.

Jealousy flashed in Albinia's eyes, and she placed a possessive hand on Squire Cavanaugh's arm. "No need for *you* to be so obliging," she said. "I can walk Roger to the door and take leave of him at the same time." And she gave the squire her arm. He promptly took it and she sailed past Beatrice, the color heightened in her cheeks, while the squire closed his eye in a wink to Beatrice. The dog trotted happily along beside them.

Beatrice watched them go, satisfied at this outcome of events. She herself wished to talk to Gareth, but she would wait until Edgar had signed his confession. Meanwhile she had one more matter to settle.

She sought the housekeeper in the kitchen, but Mrs. Teswick was not there. Rather than have her fetched, Beatrice sought her in her chamber in the servants' quarters.

The housekeeper did not hear Beatrice's knock, so Beatrice pushed the door open. Mrs. Teswick, seemingly aged a great deal in the last few hours, was packing, tears streaming down her cheeks, her bosom heaving and strangled sobs breaking from her from time to time.

Beatrice gave a loud cough.

Startled, the housekeeper turned around and stiffened, squaring her shoulders. "You wished for something, my lady?" she asked in a hoarse voice.

As Beatrice did not answer at once, she added in a tone in which hopelessness could not be concealed, "You wish to dismiss me, ma'am, of course. Turned off without references. Or . . . You won't have me arrested, will you?"

"No, Mrs. Teswick. And I shan't quite turn you off, either."

The housekeeper's legs could support her no longer. She lowered herself onto the bed; then, recalling propriety, she rose immediately.

Beatrice waved her back. "Sit down, pray." She

pushed the door to, came and stared at the housekeeper long and hard. "Do you still hate me, Mrs. Teswick?" she finally asked.

The older woman slowly shook her head. "What would be the use? He wouldn't have married Ca . . . Miss Swinton anyway. But I deluded myself for a time, thinking that it might still be possible. It was difficult for me to see you in the place that was to have been hers . . . that we all *thought* would be hers. And it should have been," she suddenly burst out with pain in her voice. "It should have been."

"You care for her very much, don't you?"

The housekeeper nodded.

"I know she is your niece," said Beatrice. And as alarm spread over the housekeeper's features, she added, "That secret is safe with me. But I do not think you can continue as a housekeeper at the manor," she further said.

Mrs. Teswick said dully, "I fancied that. That's why I am packing. I collect you shan't give me any references. Not that that would matter much, because—"

"Because your eyesight is poor and you are advanced in years," Beatrice said gently.

Fear and dismay leapt to Mrs. Teswick's eyes. "You know?"

"Yes, I know. But that secret is also safe with me. I propose a solution to you, Mrs. Teswick. I shall ask Lord Brook to set you up in a cottage on the moor as one of his tenants, a sort of semiretirement, and you could come and help us in the event of large parties and balls. That is, if you wish it so. But you need not ever worry where your next meal will be coming from. You would stay on, of course, until a new housekeeper is found. That is my plan, or if you wish to go to Ireland, to be with Camilla if she survives, we can arrange that too, and provide enough funds to keep you well in your old age."

The housekeeper stared at Beatrice with disbelieving eyes. She wished to say something, but the words became strangled in her throat. Then, to Beatrice's astonishment, she sank to her knees, grasped Beatrice's hand, and kissed it, tears still streaming down her cheeks. "Thank you, thank you, my lady," she finally managed to whisper in a hoarse voice. "God bless you for your kind and understanding heart." She sniffed, gulped, and stood up. Beatrice had to help her, for suddenly she had become a frail old woman.

Without realizing it, Mrs. Teswick lowered herself onto the bed again. "I'm sorry, I'm sorry," she wept. "I do beg your ladyship's pardon for hating you and for allowing Camilla to persuade me into shocking conduct. I deeply regret putting laudanum into the preserves. But you came to no harm. I never wished to really harm you, even when I hated you." She pushed her hand distractedly through her hair. "I don't hate you anymore. I don't feel hate . . . I don't have *any* feelings now, except sorrow," she said as if to herself.

Beatrice placed a hand briefly on her shoulder. "We all have to experience that at some time or other, but time heals all wounds, and we must always hope for the best.

"You shall let me know what it is you wish to do," she said. And left the broken old woman to her sad thoughts.

When she returned to the drawing room, Gareth was already there. "Where have you been?" he scolded her. "I was afraid you had gone on the moor alone again. It is a fine place to seek solace—for a man who knows it well, but not for you."

"Never mind the moor. Gareth, has he gone?"

"He signed the confession and will leave shortly."

"I am glad. I could not be easy with him around."

"Beatrice . . ." He came closer, hesitated, then lifted his arms to embrace her. Beatrice pushed him gently away. "Gareth, I must know this. Roger said I should ask you. Who are this mysterious woman and the child who is your heir? Is he yours?"

The baron shook his head, and Beatrice felt suddenly as if a weight had been lifted off her heart. Bastards were a common occurrence, but she did not wish her husband to have been so deeply involved with a woman as to father her child. "Then whose is it?"

"My cousin's."

Abruptly Beatrice recalled. "The one who died at Waterloo?"

He nodded, his eyes clouding for a moment with pain. "He married on his last furlough. It was not a marriage that the family would have approved of. He had no time to broach the subject with them, no time to stand buffer between his wife and the family. He had hoped to do that the next time he came home."

Gareth's lips pressed into a thin line of pain. "Only there was to be no next time.

"On his deathbed he begged me to look after his widow. I promised. Neither of us knew at the time that she was with child. I was wounded at Waterloo and was quite ill for some time, so I could not fulfill my promise right away. As soon as I could, I sought her out, at first using the squire as a messenger. Then I discovered there was an issue of the marriage. But I was not strong enough to protect Eloise from Albinia, and even then I must have had my suspicions about Edgar and did not wish her exposed to him.

"Then . . . then . . ." He took a deep breath and said in a colorless voice, "Then I broke off my engagement to Camilla. The atmosphere at Brook Manor became strained. I was cut by my friends. Not the right time to fetch a delicate mother and a child to the manor. But most important"—his lips pressed into a grim line—"I did not wish her to be subjected to Edgar's charm. He could have turned her up sweet to the extent she might have agreed to marry him. I . . . I offered her the protection of my name, but she said she could not contemplate marriage with any other man. Perhaps if I were a different man . . . But I'm not an easy person to live with, as you have discovered."

He took another deep breath. "Then I hit upon a notion. My cousin always loved Tavis Hall. He, of all the Risborough children, was the favorite of my grandfather, Sir Guy. I would inherit the estate and then give it over to Eloise and the child. She then could take her rightful place in society, without being obliged to live at Brook Manor.

"Captain Tremblay had the mistaken notion that I did not wish to acknowledge her. He threatened me. Roger hit upon the idea of inviting her to the party when he heard the captain threatening again to make a scandal. Tremblay said he would wait no longer. I but waited to secure the estate for her and see it in order."

"Was she the guest who was late?" asked Beatrice.

"Yes. I did not wish the captain to reveal the truth yet, not after the attempt on my life and with the killer running loose. I was afraid for the child, who is my heir. But now we need be afraid no longer.

"Beatrice . . ." He wished to take her in his arms, but instead he took her face in his hands and stared at her long and intently. "Beatrice," he said in a hoarse voice, "can you bring yourself to forgive me? All the dreadful things I have said to you?"

"Yes, for I shall have the memory of your saving my life—twice—to help me forgive. Forgive and forget." And now she felt with a certainty she *would* forgive and forget.

"Beatrice," he cried. "Oh, my love. I shall try to make amends, and I shall cherish you all my life."

Abruptly he paled as he saw her frown. "What is it, dear heart? Is forgiving me too difficult a task, after all?"

"No. Gareth, you must promise me *never* to ride or drive in that neck-or-nothing fashion again. I should like it to be a very long life."

"Oh, my angel," the baron said huskily, and swept her into his arms.

Beatrice threw her arms around his neck and abandoned herself to a thoroughly satisfactory kiss. Only Pedmore's entering the chamber and quickly backing off into a side table recalled them to their surroundings.

"This place is far too public for our purposes. We need more privacy. I shall carry you to my chamber," Lord Brook said, and picked her up in his arms.

"Gareth, put me down. You shouldn't—"

"I am strong enough to make it to my chamber, never fear," his lordship said, gazing at her with tenderness and love.

Beatrice threw her arms around his neck once more, and relaxing against his strong shoulder, abandoned herself to the exhilarating expectation of a truly married life.

About the Author

MIRANDA CAMERON was born in Europe. As a child, she and her parents moved to Canada, where she eventually graduated from the University of Toronto. A pharmacist, Ms. Cameron wrote as a hobby for many years before deciding to give up her career and become a professional writer. In her leisure, she enjoys painting, sculpting, reading, gardening, and traveling.